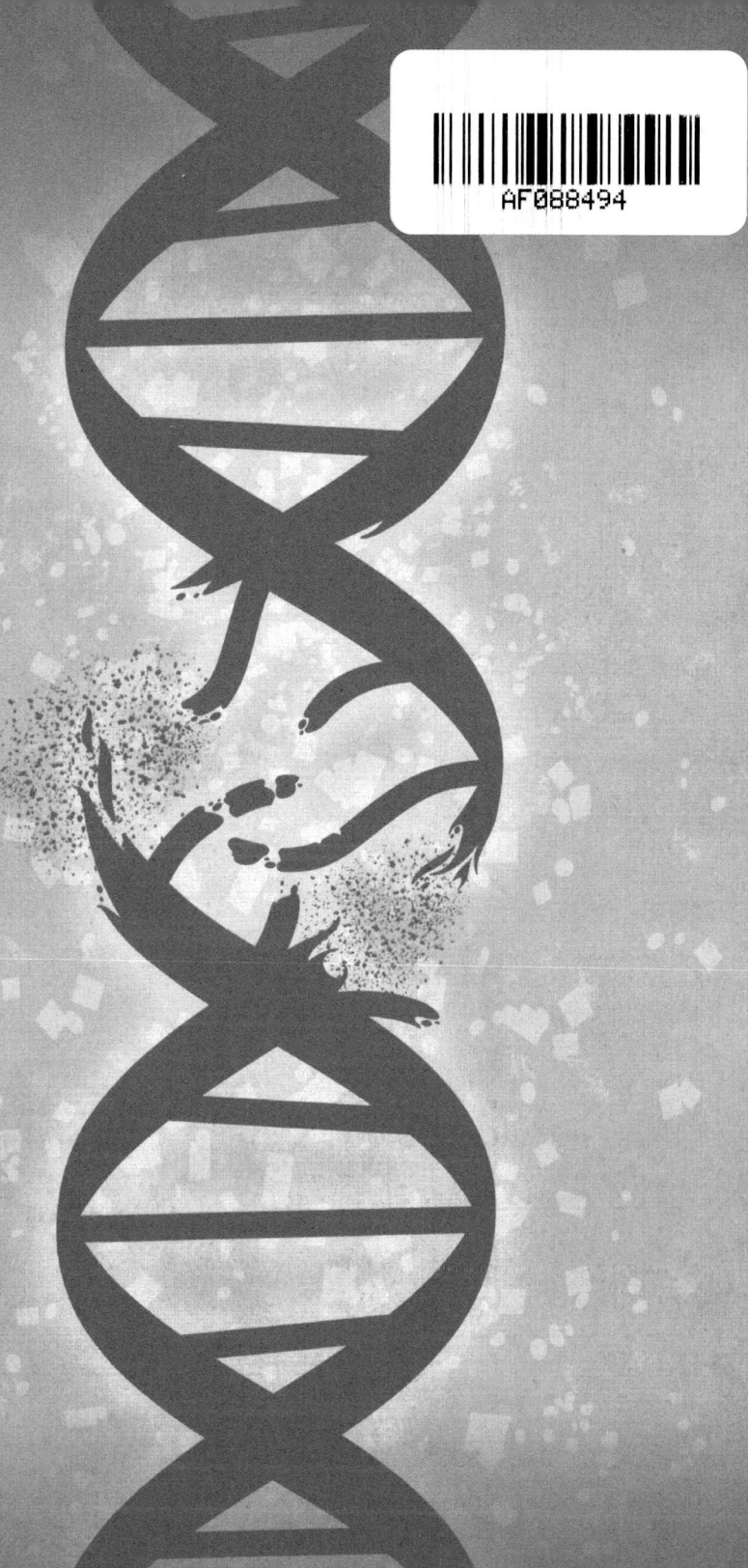

By the Same Author

Novels
Howell Grange (2019)
Gemini Day (2021)
The Densham Do 2022)
Diamond Val (2023)

Poetry Collections
Raised Voices (2014)
Kaleidoscope (2017)
The Huntington Hydra (2019)

Short Story Collections
First Flame (2013)
Odds Against (2017)
The Guy Thing (2018)
Fallen Eagles (2021)
Roxanne Riding Hood (2023)

Further details at:
www.bruceleonardharris.com

THE JUDAS GENE

BRUCE HARRIS

The Book Guild Ltd

First published in Great Britain in 2024 by
The Book Guild Ltd
Unit E2 Airfield Business Park,
Harrison Road, Market Harborough,
Leicestershire. LE16 7UL
Tel: 0116 2792299
www.bookguild.co.uk
Email: info@bookguild.co.uk
X: @bookguild

Copyright © 2024 Bruce Harris

The right of Bruce Harris to be identified as the author of this
work has been asserted by them in accordance with the
Copyright, Design and Patents Act 1988.

All rights reserved. No part of this publication may be
reproduced, transmitted, or stored in a retrieval system, in any form or by any means,
without permission in writing from the publisher, nor be otherwise circulated in
any form of binding or cover other than that in which it is published and without
a similar condition being imposed on the subsequent purchaser.

This work is entirely fictitious and bears no resemblance to any persons living or dead.

Typeset in 11pt Adobe Garamond Pro

Printed and bound in the UK by TJ Books LTD, Padstow, Cornwall

ISBN 978 1916668 935

British Library Cataloguing in Publication Data.
A catalogue record for this book is available from the British Library.

CONTENTS

PART ONE	Enigma	1
PART TWO	Exile	101
PART THREE	Awakening	141
PART FOUR	Resolution	165
PART FIVE	Aftermath	193

PART ONE

ENIGMA

Wholly illogical as he knew it was, Detective Chief Superintendent John Gregson had identified a "political ring" to his phone, whenever a politician of whatever persuasion was on the other end of the line. He regarded politicians as a form of harassment, tending to be all the more galling because there didn't seem to be much he could do about it. Telling a politico to go boil his head could invite grief of various types and intensities, but what he most resented about them was the way they seemed to creep ever more obtrusively into his life as he acquired seniority.

When I was a sergeant sweating away on a mountain of admin, I don't suppose there was a politician in the country who gave a tinker's cuss what I was doing from one day to the next. At chief inspector, I had local so-called worthies sticking their bob's worth in at every opportunity, and these days, I spend half my life talking to so and sos with political letters after their names, though I know well enough what letters I'd like to put after their name.

The phone made that familiar noise, and DCS Gregson turned an expectant eye on it.

'Hello, Chief Superintendent Gregson. This is the Attorney General speaking.'

Gregson might have laughed scornfully and told the mischievous journo on the other end of the line to leave it out, had he not met the current Attorney General Philip Coulson and knew his precise, rather nasal voice. There was always the possibility of it being a journo fancying himself as an impressionist; the A.G.'s schoolmaster tones were not too difficult to imitate. But Gregson was a believer in discretion being the better part of valour.

'Mr. Coulson, hello. What can I do for you?'

'You're not going to like it, Gregson, but I'm afraid we have something of an embarrassment on what I suppose you'd call your manor. Do you still call it that, or have I been watching too many bad cop movies?'

'It's as good a term as ever, I suppose, sir. Which part of my manor are we talking about?'

'Houghton Hall. The country home of Sir Ralph Manningham, noted industrialist and generous donor to party funds, specifically our party funds.'

Gregson was already getting the feeling he often had with politicians, which is suddenly finding himself in a room with the walls closing in on him.

'Yes, sir, I know it. One of the finest houses in the county. What seems to be the trouble?'

'Sir Ralph was found dead at six thirty this morning. One of his minions went to wake him, but he wasn't in bed. He was in his study, slumped over the desk. Half-empty bottle of pills at his side.'

Yes, I might have known it, Gregson thinks. *There is the bird above, and here is its mess all over my head.*

'Have the local police been informed?'

'Yes; I believe there are several local plods there now, making sure no one messes anything about. Until you or your appointed man gets there, of course.'

Gregson sighed inwardly.

'On the surface of it, sir, it sounds like a fairly clear case of suicide, something which an inspector in that area could probably adequately deal with.'

'No, Gregson, absolutely bloody not. No, no and no.'

'Sir?'

'I'm more or less acting as the PM's emissary here, Gregson. If Manningham has topped himself, we will need to know why before the hacks are all over it like a rash, which I don't doubt they are already heading towards. If it's money, or sex, or gambling, just about whatever in fact, it could damage the interests of the party, and in this case that more or less means the Government, very badly. We need someone with the nous and the discretion to handle it quietly. The PM does not want to wake up any morning soon and find himself looking at headlines along the lines of "Tory donor was drug dealer" or "Donations to party funds came from trafficking under-age girls". We need to find a competent guy of at least inspector rank, put him on the case exclusively so that none of his other work gets in the way, and when we know from him exactly what we're dealing with, we can handle any wider implications.'

Gregson coughed a little, a sure sign that the medicine he was having to take didn't suit.

'Putting any officer of that rank on to one case exclusively is very difficult, Mr. Coulson. We are not restored to full complement after the many recent cuts resulting from government policy. Sir.'

The last word was clearly an afterthought, and Coulson was nettled.

'Now don't be bloody awkward, Gregson. I know you're not a million miles from retirement, and I don't doubt you're already looking forward to putting your feet up in the south of France, or wherever takes your fancy. A big stink emanating from your bloody manor or whatever you call it is definitely not what you want. If you rock the party's boat, Gregson, the party will rock yours.'

For a moment, several crisp phrases reverberated in Gregson's brain. *Lead me not into temptation*, he thought. Not only would uttering a selection of them give him immense personal satisfaction, but it could also actually make his retirement, at the moment two years away, come even closer. Rocking the party boat, dangerous as it could be, might be the ideal way to ensure the approaching comfortable life approached ever more rapidly.

Or not, of course. It could also mean sliding back down the greasy pole, with a consequent reduction in pension and a good lady wife who would never forgive him for as long as they both survived.

'Are you still bloody there, Gregson?' The nasal tone evaporated, the chief superintendent noted, when the Right Honourable Coulson got a bit worked up.

'Yes, sir. I was just taking a moment to think about who the best man for the job might be. Not a lot of our officers could be said to have sensitive political antennae. I might need to take soundings, sir.'

'Well, take them quickly. When the hacks get hold of it, a Tory-donor corpse at Houghton Hall, they're going to be clustering round there like so many bloody vultures. Choose your guy and get his backside down there, Gregson, because if the *Sun* or the *Mail* are there before he is, the PM is going to be looking for heads to roll, with yours first on the block.'

At moments like this, thought Gregson, the chain of command came into its own, or to express it rather more basically, the ticking device was handed on so that the man at the top was not holding it when it went bang. He could remember Detective Superintendent Hollins saying at his interview how much he relished taking responsibility, especially in times of crisis. Now he could have an assignment which might teach him a valuable lesson, as in he who talked bollocks at interviews was like he who pissed into the wind; they got their own back.

However, rather irritatingly, Hollins seemed to have an immediate and ready answer.

'I would give the job to Inspector Bellamy, sir. It's right up his street.'

Hollins smiled confidently, partly because he was enjoying the moment. He could almost bet his house that Gregson didn't know who he was talking about, in spite of the fact that Max Bellamy was, by police standards, a famous man. Gregson had only been in post for five years, after all, but he had spent most of it sat in his office, with, in the opinions of many of his minions, his thumb up his bum.

'Yes, right, Inspector Bellamy. Of course. Just remind me, Tom, why you would select him particularly?'

Hollins thought about keeping a tease going a little; it was one of his hobby horses that the type of guy who often rose to high office in the Force was likely to be a yes man with all the imagination of a caravan site. They were the only ones guaranteed not to bother anyone, so their promotion was no threat to anyone either.

But now that he had reached some quite dizzying heights himself, it was an argument which ultimately defeated itself. *Play it straight*, his tactful voice whispered in his ear.

'Bellamy is an unusual policeman, sir. He's loaded, mainly on his own account from inherited money, but also on his wife's. He is much more likely to move in the kind of circles frequented by Manningham, and he's up to every hack trick because he used to be one himself. His wife still is.'

'I see.'

'She could perhaps more accurately be described as his co-habitee, sir. No one seems to have any recollection of them ever actually marrying. But yes, she's a journalist, if not exactly the muck-raking type. More environmental. The quality, not the tabloids.'

'So this is a rich man, apparently with a rich wife, or partner, or whatever she is. And he's also a serving police officer. And does he do as he's told, Hollins?'

'More or less, sir. Though once he has it in his head that he's right, he can take a lot of shifting. I've heard that he changed from journalism to police work because he didn't want to just investigate the bad guys, he wanted to actually send them down. He's been known to complain that the forces of the law didn't necessarily act as quickly as they should have done when he was on to someone as a hack.'

'He doesn't necessarily come across to me as an officer with the tact and diplomacy we need for this job, Tom.'

Hollins stared at the man on his screen for a moment, relishing the words just spoken, as he remembered that DCS Gregson's legendary lack of tact and diplomacy had already landed the Force with several awkward media moments, and he was now sometimes referred to by the rank and file as "Good Grief Gregson".

'Perhaps I have slightly misrepresented him, sir. Because of his affluent background and his many eminent contacts, he is probably the nearest thing to a professional diplomat that our Force possesses. I make reference to his opinions as expressed in private to me, but that's as a result of a long-standing friendship.'

'I see. In that case, Tom, perhaps you might be in a better position to approach him than I am. But you must impress on him that, for the duration of this case, however short or long it may be, he must work on it and it alone.'

Lovely footwork, Mr. Gregson, Hollins thought. *Now I find myself in the position of having to tell Maximilian Bellamy what to do. Lucky me.*

Inspector Bellamy himself was at home at that moment, in his study, a room rather larger than studies generally tend to be. Visitors to the house would sometimes refer to it as his "library", and in truth it was a generous room, occupying most of the front right quarter of the house. In Georgian days, the room would have represented the area most commonly used to welcome and entertain distinguished guests, but Mr. Bellamy and his co-habitee, Louise Mendel, had a rather more utilitarian attitude to the spaces they owned.

Bellamy himself would not have called it his library, large and well-appointed as it was, for reasons of modesty as much as anything else. "Modest" was not generally a word many people who knew him would use; he was widely seen as more or less entirely unflappable, and having an extraordinary gift for finding a way to be accepted in almost any company he might keep, which these days tended to include some on both extremes of society – the very affluent and the very poor, the very confident and the very unsure, the very welcoming and the very hostile.

He was currently examining the layout of a Victorian house which he strongly suspected was being used for illicit purposes, possibly including trafficking. Within a couple of days, he was due to lead a raid on the place, and the intelligence he had suggested it was quite possible that some of the inmates might be armed. This last detail he had not told Louise. Bellamy regarded all information as a commodity, to be banked and released only when absolutely necessary.

Sitting with one leg thrown over the other while holding the drawings of the house open in front of him, he was not a figure who most neutral observers would conclude was a policeman. Slightly built and elegantly dressed, even if the dress amounted to no more than a neat, open-necked white shirt and some well-pressed light grey trousers, he was just under six feet tall and, but for the slight tinges of grey in the temples and a few faint lines under the eyes, he could easily have passed as a male model taking his ease before the next photo session.

However, at closer quarters that impression would be belied by the eyes. Bellamy's eyes, always wide open and always startlingly blue, could produce a whole repertoire of reactions in the people he met, including people with something to hide immediately wanting to unburden themselves to him and people with problems to solve deciding he might be the one to help them find solutions.

When concentrating, as he was now, the eyes were alive to the point of intensity, partly because, when alone, Bellamy had no reason to regulate their use. Although he was not a vain man, he was aware of the potential uses of his eyes and could adapt them for various purposes ranging from empathy to interrogation.

At the moment, he was working out in his mind how a team of five people could enter a substantial Victorian house with the least possible danger to themselves. Much as Bellamy was sometimes considered a rather cerebral policeman, he could apply his mind to highly practical matters when he had to, and operations involving surveillance and entry to premises of various kinds had not started with his police experience, but back in his journalistic days, when the whole business could be even more complicated because of the lack of official authorisation and support.

He was mentally going through the initial break-in to the house when his phone sounded, with no more than a few gentle burrs. Bellamy's hearing had always been acute, and he didn't believe in making unnecessary noise.

'Max Bellamy,' he said. He recognised the voice immediately. 'Oh, hello, Tom.' He knew this was not necessarily the most recognised way for an inspector to greet a call from a superintendent, but he had known Hollins in his journalistic days, and they had become friends before issues of rank entered the relationship.

Hollins put his case briefly.

'So that's the size of it, Max. Repercussions all the way up the line, to the PM himself. Panic in Whitehall. Not that any of them genuinely give a shit about Manningham; it's just when such an incident happens and starts making waves, they all want to make sure it isn't them who sinks. They want you to go there and put a lid on it; find out what's behind it all and keep it in house.'

'And what's made Gregson think that I'm the man for the job?'

'Me, Max, I'm afraid. I have to hold my hand up to that one. You know how to talk to the knobs, or at least you know better than I do. I would just get up their nose.'

'How come the local police can't handle it?'

'Because, Inspector, we are moving in very knobby circles. Manningham's widow, Brigitte Lacoste – she kept her maiden name – doesn't phone the local station, she phones her mate the Attorney General, who she probably knows from some knobby conference or something; she used to be a French politician. AG tells PM; PM tells AG hush hush is essential, see to it. AG passes it to Gregson, Gregson passes it to me, I pass it to you. It's all about who's still holding it when the music stops, and that, buddy, is you.'

'Cheers. If I was still working for the *Globe*, I'd tell you to sod off. But as it happens, I know both of them, not particularly well, but I know them. I've been to their house, if you can call the place a house; it's more like a palace in parts. Why in the hell would Manningham kill himself?'

'Who knows? It's mine to speculate and yours to find out, Max.'

'What about Elaine?'

Sergeant Elaine Price was Bellamy's sidekick and had been ever since he became an inspector.

'What about her?'

'If I'm going to do this, Tom, I need Elaine. I need Elaine whatever I'm doing. It's all very well you going on about my facility with the knobs; a lot of that is Elaine tugging my elbow and telling me to mind my language. She is also at least as clever as I am and probably better at understanding women. Attending to one case exclusively is difficult enough, but it will be even more so without Elaine. There's also this house raid we have planned in three days' time; if that doesn't happen, Tom, a lot of work tracking down this gang is going to go to waste. I know I'm a policeman now and when you say jump, I have to jump, but you know well enough life isn't like that for me, Tom, try as I might.'

'Too much money, you prima donna you. OK, Max, it's as well for you you've got someone prepared to negotiate, but I know well enough if you're pushed too far, you'll swan off back to hackland and I'll have you chasing my tail for ever afterwards, damn you. OK, I'll put someone on the raid with a team and make sure it's someone decent, and Elaine can go off with you to the knobs. Alright?'

'You are a truly enlightened policeman, Detective Superintendent Hollins.'

'Don't push it. Get back to me tomorrow and tell me what the score is.'

Bellamy immediately arranged a car and Elaine's company. Predictably, she was not happy about the raid.

'If it was anyone else but Tom Hollins, I'd be as doubtful as you are. But I know he or whoever he puts on it will make a decent job of it. And this job we've got could be a real feather in the cap, Elaine.'

'I haven't noticed you being that bothered about feathers in the cap before.'

'Means to an end. The more shiny feathers you've got showing in your cap, the less likely they are to shit on it.'

'If you say so. Am I driving?'

'If that's OK, yes. I've arranged one at the pool for you to pick up.'

'I'll be with you in about half an hour, sir.'

For a while, Bellamy sat and thought. Sitting and thinking, he always maintained, was an essential part of the job. And in the case of this particular job, that was probably even truer than usual.

He cast his mind back to the last time he'd met up with Manningham and Brigitte Lacoste. It was the kind of do which Hollins would undoubtedly describe as "knobby", a celebration dinner relating to the success of one of Manningham's ventures, something to do with renewable energy projects in the local area, which is why Louise, who was the environmental correspondent for her paper, had been invited. He had initially been reluctant to go with her.

'I'm perfectly happy to be sociable, Louise, but I can't see much I can contribute.'

'Sociable will do. We need to be two on this one, Max, not least because Ralph and Brigitte are so emphatically two. I want to be able to talk to Ralph; he's the wealthiest guy in the neighbourhood, he has a genuine concern for environmental matters, and I need to establish the relationship, on a purely professional basis, that is. While I'm doing that, you can keep Brigitte amused; by all accounts, she's a bit of an anglophile, with an especial interest in the male of the species. Hook her in with those eyes of yours. Only don't hook her in too far. Remember when you make a catch, the civilised thing is to put them back in the water.'

'Sure, and you remember it too. I don't want to see you gobbling up Manningham with a portion of chips and tartar sauce.'

In the event, the gathering included so many people that one-to-one conversation was not easy, but Manningham, Max remembered, was a conscientious and able host, who clearly was making a point of talking personally to all of his twenty-odd guests at some stage of the evening. Max had taken a glass of a very good white wine, whatever it was, out on to the terrace in front of the hall, partly to enjoy some fresh air after the rather fuggy warmth inside, and partly to think about yet another county-lines case needing attention.

He heard a soft, clearing-the-throat sort of cough, and turned to see Manningham standing beside him.

'Inspector Bellamy or Max?' he said.

'Max on this occasion, as I'm not on duty. At least, I hope I'm not on duty.'

'So do I. As far as I know, my activities are all comfortably within the limits of the law, even the much-publicised donations to the Conservative Party.'

'Your money, your business. I'm not St Peter, and these are not the Pearly Gates.'

'My god.' Manningham pretended to shudder. 'The idea of St Peter being a socialist avenger is a daunting one indeed. That's not a heaven I would particularly want to inhabit. However, much as the media like to go on about those donations, they don't amount to very much, to be honest, and they're more in the spirit of distractions than anything very ideological. If you see a pack of jackals in your vicinity, it makes sense to chuck them a bit of meat to chew over, which lessens the chances of them making a meal out of you.'

'I suppose so.'

Max noticed that he was actually slightly taller than Manningham, contrary to the impression he had when they were sitting at the dinner table. Which suggested that Manningham used something on his chair to make him look taller than he was. That, and the immediate denunciation of the significance of his party donations, suggested an element of insecurity, a man who needed not only to bolster his size in public, but deflect criticism from some of his political activities. Bellamy knew something of the brittleness of supposedly successful men from both his journalistic and police experience, but he'd also known men whose lives had ended in suicide, and the impression of Manningham he came away with that day – sensitive and image conscious, but not immediately vulnerable – did not suggest that suicide would be his fate.

They talked for a while, and Manningham was soon on what Max suspected was his favourite topic, the science of human survival in general and climate change in particular. Max had done a certain amount of homework in his library; men who Louise thought worthy of a "relationship", even if not of the romantic kind, were men he felt he needed to know something about.

Manningham's father had been the founder and manager of a company making household aids of the pre-computer era, including early vacuum cleaners, carpet shampooers, old-fashioned clothes washing equipment and the like. The literature on the subject strongly suggested that Ralph, the son and heir, had unsubtly, if not brutally, taken over the business, put the old man out to grass, and then taken it in directions which were both logical developments and others not so logical. His father had only survived his retirement by a few years. As he made conversation with Manningham, inconsequential as it was in the main, Max gained a certain impression of ruthlessness, and a feeling that when the other man made remarks about throwing meat to the Conservative jackals, he was only half joking, and he did ultimately suspect that some of his activities might be viewed as dubious by them.

Max had also briefly met Manningham's partner, Brigitte Lacoste, but there were three people present at the time, including Max's partner, Louise, and most of the conversation was between the two women. However, that did enable him to form an impression without having to make too much conversation himself, which temperamentally suited him, and the impression he got was of a forceful, eloquent and assertive woman who wore her dual nationality more easily than many people would do in a similar situation. Although brought up and educated in France, Brigitte had an English mother, and she spoke English virtually without any accent at all. The wariness which many people would have when they knew Bellamy was a policeman didn't seem present in Brigitte Lacoste at all, perhaps partly because her responsibilities in the French Parliament had for a time included being a junior minister in the department dealing with law and order, when dealing with lawyers, police personnel, judges, etc., would have been a daily occurrence.

Since then, he had come across both the Manninghams a few more times; they lived in the same county, and the local who's who was not large or extensive. Usually, it was in the context of a meeting or conference with political or legal implications – Brigitte's journalistic speciality related to both British and European law and their political interpretations. Brigitte was as capable of making sensible comments on some MP or minister's extra-marital affairs as she was of analysing the likely impact of some new legislation.

As he brooded on the Manninghams, Elaine was concentrating on her driving, and it took Max some minutes into the journey before he realised that Elaine was disgruntled. He was also too honest with himself to deny that she did have a few things to be disgruntled about, since she had done a good deal of the spadework research and preparation work for the upcoming house raid. Bellamy moved easily from one subject to the next and often expected people he worked with to do likewise; it wasn't always that easy.

So now he had a problem. Not for a moment did he imagine that Elaine would let her mood interfere with the efficiency of her work, but Bellamy's pronounced sense of basic justice did tell him that she was entitled to much more explanation than she had had so far. Both condescending and imperative tones would be inappropriate now, so he searched his mind for the right words and approach.

'Tom Hollins told me, not long before you turned up, that he was going to lead the raid himself,' he said. 'He said he was going to ask you to gen him up. Did he do that?'

'Sort of.' Elaine's eyes remained firmly on the road. 'But I'd drafted out a copy of the plan, taking into account what you said about it, and I passed that on as well.'

'I'm sorry, Elaine. It's all a bit rushed and high-handed. But it came down to me from Olympus itself, believe me. There's panic in very high places about this Manningham business, and if anyone's going to get bladdered first, it's going to be us, the infantry.'

'Is, or should I say was, Manningham that important to them, then, sir?'

'Apparently. Partly because of the donations to party funds, of course, but I think there's more to it than that. Manningham's one of their blue-eyed boys; rich as Croesus, self-made man—'

'Self-made? He inherited a fortune, didn't he?'

'Oh, yes, but that doesn't necessarily disqualify you from blue-eyed-boy status in government circles. You're self-made if you've done something sensible with it, rather than blown the lot on wine and women. Or beer and boys, whatever's your preference. Manningham took all the money his dad made, modernised the business and ticked all the boxes – providing employment, ramping up exports, doing research and development. His knighthood was probably in the pipeline.'

'So whatever it was that made him do away with himself was probably something pretty fruity, for him to chuck all that up?'

'Yes, assuming he did do away with himself.'

Elaine never swivelled her eyes away from the road when she was driving, but she'd put out clues anyway, should she feel herself gobsmacked by something, and her eyebrows shot up to the top of her head.

'So you don't think this necessarily is suicide, sir?'

'Until I've been there and had a good look at everything, I don't come to any conclusions. I've told you before about my fat alcoholic mentor of distant days, an old editor called, with a nice touch of irony, Shepherd. 'If it looks like a duck, smells like a duck and moves like a duck, then yes, it's probably a duck, but that doesn't stop it being a duck with a grenade inside it.'

As they drove up the driveway to Houghton Hall, impressive and obviously meant to be impressive, they found themselves slightly intimidated, however indifferent they set out to be to grandeur and display. Bellamy was trying to visualise himself making this journey with the aim of arresting one of the wealthy inhabitants of the house when he got there. He had already worked out that the reason he was on this case must have been the result of someone in this house making a call to some very exalted personage indeed, probably a government minister. Hollins had been summoned from on high, in the shape of DCS Gregson, so whoever this was could take upon himself the right to tell detective chief superintendents what to do.

Eventually, after what seemed like a tour of the local woodland, the car drew up in front of the majestic facade of Houghton Hall. Bellamy pressed a small bell on a remarkably large door, and as he turned to Elaine beside him, she rolled her eyes slowly at him.

'Seriously posh gaff, sir. We'd better wipe our feet.'

Bellamy grinned back at her, and the expression was still on his face as it became obvious that the door was being opened, if somewhat laboriously. However, before whoever was behind it came into view, the grin was wiped away. They were shortly to be in the presence of death, and there was little or nothing that Bellamy respected more than death.

Gradually, and almost apologetically, the tall figure of a young man, still not long out of boyhood, appeared. His hair was blondish and swept back, his shoulders resembled a champion swimmer, and his dress verged on the formal, with a shirt and tie and what looked like suit trousers.

Bellamy showed his warrant card, and the young man didn't appear to need to get any closer to it. He gave Elaine's an even more casual glance, and then turned to shout to someone in the main body of the house, but he hadn't actually opened his mouth before the someone in question appeared.

'OK, Paul, thank you, I'll take it from here.'

Brigitte Lacoste crossed the generous expanse of hall in a few seconds. She looked tired and harassed, but she was still a remarkably attractive woman, even in no more than a pair of jeans and a blue smock covering her top half. The wide greenish eyes took in the couple now standing inside the door, and she made an attempt to smile; at that moment, Bellamy's heart went out to her. He didn't know her particularly well, but what he did know of her suggested to him that she deserved more than to get up on a day like all other days and suddenly find her husband had killed himself. Supposedly, perhaps, but devastating enough, nevertheless. Yet another doubt about the supposed suicide resounded in his head; how many men would really want to rid themselves of such a woman?

'We call Paul a butler, which is very grand and, of course, ridiculously anachronistic, but in truth he's a jack of all trades, in spite of his age, and master of a surprising number of them. I suppose a better term would be aide-de-camp; French can be very useful when a certain precision is needed. We have most of the family gathered here now; my stepdaughter, Anne, Ralph's daughter from his first marriage to Mary Willows, was visiting anyway, along with her husband, Damien. My stepson, Anne's brother, Miles, and his wife, Rachel, who live about thirty miles away, came as soon as I contacted them. Anyway, that's enough information to overload you with for the time being, Max, so welcome to Houghton Hall; once again, in your case, Max, though I don't know the lady with you.'

'Sergeant Elaine Price, this is Madame Brigitte Lacoste, the lady of the house,' Bellamy said.

'Pleased to meet you,' said Elaine.

Bellamy could see that Elaine was doing her usual visual precis of the other woman. In spite of Brigitte's remarkable self-possession in the circumstances, her state of mind was suddenly very visible as she turned sideways on and Bellamy saw her in profile; the eyes, he saw, were still a little misted and the clothing was dishevelled, which, Bellamy thought, was probably highly uncharacteristic.

'I'm deeply sorry to have to make a visit in these circumstances, Brigitte,' he said.

Brigitte nodded and momentarily seemed about to weep, but Bellamy witnessed the emotional effort she made and appreciated that this was not a woman who easily lost control.

'I had hoped they would send you, Max, since I knew you were sort of local. That man Coulson is not my favourite politico in the world – I don't have many favourite politicos, to be honest – but I do know him from my own political days and what good are levers if you don't pull them now and then? At the moment, we have a local sergeant guarding the scene of the crime, if that's what it is, and I think he's a bit out of his depth, to be honest. But he and his constable have done what they needed to do, to be fair; everything is as it was, and they've studiously avoided putting their paw prints all over the place.'

The last two sentences of this speech were thrown behind her as Brigitte led the way to the downstairs right side of the house, where the little group first passed through an impressive living room, all the more striking for its relative lightness of touch and pastel colours, and on into a more studious-looking space, with shelves on three sides of the room packed with books and folders, and a rather incongruous large mahogany desk, behind which Ralph Manningham was still sitting, his head down on a writing pad in front of him and a small bottle of pills next to it, with some of the pills spilling out.

Bellamy recognised the local sergeant, Rob Denham; Denham had only a few years to go before retirement after thirty years' service, and, while imagination and creativity were probably not his strong suits, he was utterly reliable and would undoubtedly have done everything which at this stage needed doing, though Bellamy was too old a hand to take that for granted.

Two plain-clothes guys were busy taking photos of the scene and carefully inspecting the room for anything which might be relevant. Bellamy saw that outside the room, on a generously sized patio, a very young constable was keeping watch in case of any media intrusions or unexpected visitors. It seemed that someone had managed to keep the news away from the media so far, for which Bellamy was grateful; the situation as it stood was going to be difficult enough.

'Hello, Rob,' he said. 'Are we all in order? Arrangements made for the body to be collected, post-mortem, death certificate, etc.?'

'All in order, sir.' The sergeant glanced rather dubiously at Brigitte gazing forlornly into the room without entering it, and Bellamy realised that he needed to give Brigitte something to do, and temporarily remove her from this spot.

'Brigitte, I would be most grateful if you could gather together everyone who is in the house at the moment in whichever room is most convenient for meeting up. I will need to talk to everyone, and it would save time and effort if it could be everyone at once. Elaine,' he said, turning to her, 'could you go with Brigitte and help in whatever way you can, and then come back and tell me when everything is ready. I will need at least fifteen to twenty minutes.'

As the two women disappeared, Bellamy turned to the sergeant.

'OK, Rob, what's the score? How long have we got?'

'They're ready to collect the body when we are. ASAP, they say, sir.'

'Do they now? OK, we'll do our best. And we have a post-mortem organised?'

'As soon as you OK it, sir.'

'And you've got the lad there posted, I see. I don't recognise him.'

'Chris Spencer, sir. Twenty-one years old. I think this is his first suicide. I thought he'd be better off out there; in any case, we'll have the media descending on us quite soon now, and he's our early warning system.'

At the moment, Bellamy saw the young man on the patio suddenly freeze, and while he didn't have the view of the drive that the constable did, he guessed that Spencer had just seen at least one vehicle approaching. Bellamy immediately turned to see if there would be a similar reaction in the house. At that moment, the young man Paul hove into view, and his appearance was immediately followed by an odd gesture, his hands clasping together as if in anxiety. Bellamy suspected the room Paul had just been in was the one looking out over the approach road to the hall entrance, and he wondered why Paul would be anxious at the sight of approaching cars. Of course, the man was very young, and this sudden death could itself cause such a reaction, but Bellamy found himself speculating that it may have been Paul who had contacted the media, for whatever purposes of his own. Bellamy hoped it wasn't about selling a story.

The immediate need was to examine the body and the room around it. Bellamy walked up to the table and looked down. He could see that the bottle which still contained a few pills was unmarked, meaning that how many pills were supposed to be in it would be difficult to calculate. The pills themselves were small and orange-coloured, and Bellamy found himself comparing them to some very similar ones taken by his seventy-eight-year-old mother; hers were called atenolol and they were standard beta blockers, aimed at helping with blood pressure and angina. Manningham was known to have heart problems, and it was quite credible that he would take these pills. But, while they would not do a patient a lot of good if taken in large numbers and would probably induce weakness, a very slow heart rate and probably shortness of breath, he doubted whether they would be sufficient to kill. And Bellamy guessed that if the pills spilled over the desk were added to those inside the bottle, the number was probably not far short of what should be in the bottle.

For a long time, Bellamy stood looking at the desk, the body and the scattered pills. He started to mentally tick off on his fingers the various possible explanations for what he was seeing. If

Manningham was making a last-ditch attempt to save his life after a severe heart episode, it would mean that he would have to think that these things had the capacity to save his life, and Bellamy doubted very much whether Manningham the advanced scientist would believe such a thing. If the whole scene was an attempt to simulate a suicide, it was an extraordinarily naïve and crude one, and one which suggested a panic reaction rather than a calculated intention. But who could possibly be desperate to convince whoever inspected this scene that Manningham committed suicide? And why on earth would anyone want to?

Bellamy checked his train of thought before it ran away on false premises. There were, of course, many pills of a similar sort of colour, and no conclusions could be made until he knew what the pills were for definite. Perhaps it was possible that someone thought the situation would be dealt with by country-bumpkin policemen who would simply conclude a suicide attempt by the appearance of how things seemed to be, but even at that level they must have realised that some kind of analysis of the pills would be carried out. The suggestion was now that someone found Manningham dead, or somehow caused him to die, and, lacking time or opportunity to concoct something better, arranged this little pantomime with the pills.

'Right.' Bellamy looked around at the forensic boys, who now seemed to have stopped taking photos. 'Have you got all you want, boys?'

They nodded.

'Anything spring to mind at this stage?' Bellamy believed in picking all the brains he could.

'It's difficult to see with the naked eye, sir, but something's scuffed up that carpet, from the point where it borders the patio to the chair where the guy is sitting. Take the camera in closer, and it's just about visible. It's possible that he took his chair out onto the patio and then brought it back in, but would he be up to heaving chairs about just before whatever happened, happened? And the marks anyway suggest something more substantial than a chair.'

Looking through the camera's close-up sights, Bellamy could see what was being described, an undoubted and fairly recent disturbance of the carpet.

'OK, point noted. Well spotted. Now, Rob,' he said, turning back to the sergeant, 'can we get those pills off to someone who can tell us what they are? I have an idea, but I'm not doing anything with it until I have them confirmed, whatever they are.'

Elaine had suddenly manifested herself in the doorway of the room.

'Everyone gathered and waiting, sir.'

'OK, Elaine, I'm on my way. I want that lad Paul there too.'

'He's not there at the moment, sir. I'll take you to the room, then I'll go and get him.'

'Right, and when you've done that, Elaine, prepare to repel boarders. I think some cars are coming up the drive, and if they are who I think they are, which is hacks of one kind or another, they should not on any account be allowed into the house. We will also need to reinforce that young guy outside; either you or Sergeant Denham, I think it needs to be.'

In addition to Brigitte and Paul, two men and two women were waiting for him in the most imposing room on the ground floor, which Bellamy suspected was probably once called the drawing room. Brigitte, still determined to perform her duties as a hostess, in spite of what Bellamy could see it was costing her, escorted him around the room, introducing him to each member of the family. Anne Atcliffe, Brigitte's stepdaughter, had been sitting on the sofa beside Brigitte and was therefore the first to be introduced. She was an attractive woman whose resemblance to Ralph Manningham was obvious enough, but Bellamy was a little taken aback with her welcoming expression. As a good-looking man, he was not unused to appraising looks from women, sometimes almost overtly seductive, but at this time and in this place, it was so clearly inappropriate that he was momentarily speechless. Her husband, Damien, who looked younger than his wife, sitting on an armchair next to the sofa, smiled widely and nodded; Bellamy guessed that he was not a complicated man and took most things in his stride.

In the armchair closest to the door sat a middle-aged bespectacled man, clearly tall even though he was sitting down, and wearing a frown as if he considered his time was being wasted. Brigitte introduced him as Miles Manningham, her stepson and Manningham's eldest offspring, and on a smaller chair on the other side of the room, as if detaching herself from the rest of the company, his wife, Rachel, was introduced. The young man Paul stood deferentially to one side.

The last of the introductions was only just completed when Miles Manningham spoke.

'At last, we're done with the formalities,' he said. 'Now perhaps we can get on.'

Bellamy responded amiably enough.

'Yes, ladies and gentlemen, my apologies if you have had a wait, but I'm afraid matters like this cannot be rushed, even when quick conclusions are a feasible possibility. We are talking about a man's death, and while I don't believe in hierarchies in the matter of death, this particular man is of a singular eminence and interest in what has happened here is by no means confined to this room. We do have to ensure that everything is handled properly. The lady just approaching the door there is Sergeant Elaine Price. How are we with the media, Elaine?'

'About eight or nine already, sir.'

'Right.' Bellamy noted another physical reaction from the boy Paul, who had been standing leaning against the wall, looking as if he didn't want to be there and was wondering why he'd been summoned. He suddenly stood up as if expecting something else to happen. Bellamy noted the link and put investigating it on his to-do list.

'Could you tell them that I will make a brief statement to them in about twenty minutes? In the meantime, please point out to them that they are technically trespassing simply in the act of entering the precincts of the hall without prior permission, and if any of them move away from the front car park into any other area of the premises, they will be expelled and may be prosecuted for trespassing.'

Elaine went on her errand, and almost immediately, the middle-aged man spoke again.

'With the greatest of respect to you and your office, Inspector, this is a straightforward case, surely? My father was ill with heart disease and had been for some time, and he decided to take his own life, wrongly perhaps, but understandably, nevertheless. Such an event is already traumatic enough for the family, isn't it, without extra noise and fuss being made of it?'

Bellamy mentally ticked off the notable features, such as they were. The man was thinning on top, but he still had a largely black mop of slightly dishevelled hair; his eyes, glinting at Bellamy through large spectacles, spoke of a certain detachment, and even arrogance, and his jumper and shirt suggested the businessman dressed for a weekend at home. He was sitting upright in the armchair and Bellamy estimated he was probably well over six feet tall.

Bellamy settled himself in an armchair on the other side of the room from the man before replying.

'You are Mr. Manningham's son, I gather?'

'Yes. I am the eldest son of the gentleman I suppose we must now call the deceased. I speak for no one but myself, but I personally would like to be allowed to begin my mourning for a great man.'

Here, his voice temporarily broke, and his head dropped. Bellamy, without allowing his eyes to leave Manningham, could see that he did not seem to be commanding much empathy from the other people in the room.

'I am sorry, sir, for your loss, and sorry again that I have to disagree with you. I have reason to believe that what has happened in this house may not be as straightforward as it seems, and my job here is to find the truth.'

'It is obvious what has happened here, Inspector.'

'Oh, do shut up, Miles,' said his wife from the far side of the room, who, until now, it seemed, had been holding her silence with some difficulty. She was a harassed-looking woman, probably in her mid-forties, whose eyes were suddenly alight with anger. She was dressed very casually, with minimal make-up, as if the call to her in-laws' house had arrived early and out of the blue.

'I am Rachel Manningham, the wife of the gentleman who has just spoken, and I am now wishing he hadn't. Miles always has to take control; I think he would even be...'

'Such is married bliss, with a partner who can always be relied on to stab one in the back at the appropriate moment...'

Bellamy got to his feet slowly, and his movement and expression were enough to re-impose silence.

'Forgive me,' he said, in a tone which clearly was not asking for anyone's forgiveness. 'This is a police investigation following the sudden death of an eminent man. I know from past experience what sudden deaths can do to families, and it is clearly having a traumatic effect on yours. However, I have a duty to perform and not an unlimited amount of time to perform it, and it is only right for me to warn you that I am quite prepared, if necessary, to charge whoever may be guilty of it with obstructing my investigation or wasting police time.'

Bellamy let his words sink in, and then resumed.

'I must insist that anyone who needs to leave this house over the next couple of days gives Sergeant Price specific information as to where they will be and when. This is an investigation, and if I were to come to any conclusions at this stage, there would be no point in an investigation. I need to talk on a one-to-one basis to everyone who was in the house at the time of Mr. Manningham's death, as well as any members of the family who have arrived since that time. I shall ask Ms. Lacoste to set me up in an appropriate room and I will talk to people without the distraction of other members of the family present. Please remain in the house or in the grounds until I have seen you. Brigitte, may I have a word?'

Bellamy moved out of the room in the direction of the front door, and Brigitte went to meet him. Silence remained in the room behind them for what Bellamy regarded as a gratifyingly long time.

Brigitte spoke even before Bellamy asked her the direct question.

'We have three apartments on the east side of the house which we use for guests and occasionally for holiday lets, Max. I know one of them is empty this week, but they are kept in a decent condition whether they are occupied or vacant. It is effectively soundproof; most of the walls of this place are at least two feet thick. If you'd like to come with me now, I will set you up there and send your sergeant to you while I man the main entrance.'

Bellamy looked at her gratefully. In situations like these, at least one member of the family needed to keep their head, and Brigitte was clearly doing so.

'Thank you, Brigitte. You lead, I'll follow.'

The apartment was, of course, ideal for the purpose. Immaculately clean and comfortably furnished, it did not in any way resemble an office or an interview room, which was fine as far as Max was concerned. He was intent on investigating, not interrogating.

'Perfect, Brigitte. I appreciate you being prepared to send Sergeant Price to me, but I do feel it is necessary now to make a statement to the media, to mark their card as much as anything else. I know how they think; I am sort of poacher turned gamekeeper.'

As they made their way to the front entrance, Brigitte couldn't resist making the meaning of Max's words as clear as possible.

'You used to be a journalist?'

'Yes, I did. Between the ages of eighteen and twenty-eight, I slogged away at it, before deciding that actually catching them was more satisfying than chasing them around. I've been a policeman now for twelve years, meaning turning forty is pretty imminent, incredible as it still seems.'

'Forty is an age I can only be nostalgic about,' Brigitte said, and her smile was like a torch flash, instant and forgotten.

They reached the imposing portico entrance. Elaine was standing dourly in the middle of the doorway, and a couple of young constables were either side of the huge doors. Clearly, another carload of local police personnel had turned up, and Elaine had handled it, as she usually did.

The ladies and gentlemen of the media slowly converged on the entrance, and Bellamy noted that one or two of them were straying further away into the grounds of the house than he was comfortable with.

'Ladies and gentlemen, my name is Inspector Max Bellamy of the county force. I can confirm that Mr. Ralph Manningham, the owner of this house, died here this morning. I can say nothing much more than that at this stage, but when investigations have reached a more advanced stage, I don't doubt that I will have more to say. How long that process will take, I cannot predict at this point.

'I must emphasise that police personnel are also watching and checking on the grounds of the hall, and anyone found on them will be expelled from the estate altogether and may well be prosecuted for trespassing.'

'Just a minute,' a voice said, and Max saw a man obviously older than most of the media folk present looking at him intently.

'Max Bellamy? You used to be a journo yourself, didn't you?'

'Correct, and I'll not deny it. So, I know all the tricks, guys, so be good boys and girls and don't fuck me around. OK?'

A few slightly startled "rights" and "OK's" and Max was on his way back to the apartment chosen for his work, accompanied by Elaine and Brigitte. As they approached the door, Bellamy turned to Brigitte.

'It would seem to make sense for me to talk to you first, Brigitte, which will then release you to keep an eye on everything; do you feel up to it?'

'I was rather hoping you'd start with me. Yes, I would like to get it over with, Max; the whole thing still seems like some grotesque bad dream, but I have to keep in touch with reality somehow.'

'Thank you. Please go in and make yourself comfortable. Elaine, could you take charge of authorising the removal of the body now? We will need to get a car round to that patio outside the room where he was found; take it round the back of the house away from the media people. Let me know – by phone, don't come into the apartment here – when he's off to post-mortem, and bust the ass of any of those media people if you have to.'

'My pleasure, boss,' she said. Bellamy turned into the apartment and shut the door. As he had guessed, the lock on it was a Yale, which wouldn't open unless someone had a key.

Brigitte had chosen to sit on the main sofa in the apartment living room; it was a much more modern, airy and minimalist sort of setting than the grand lounge downstairs where the family had been sitting. To her left, the main window of the room generously illuminated her face and torso. Bellamy sat himself in an armchair to the right of the sofa, where he could see every nuance of her facial expression. He suspected that, as an ex-politician, Brigitte would know about the effects of light in interview situations, and her choice of such a position told him from the start that it was unlikely that she felt she had anything to hide.

'Brigitte, I have to start, of course, with going back to the events of last night and this morning as you remember them. I know this is likely to be an awkward and difficult experience for you, but it would help if you could take the process gradually and include as much detail as you can. It cannot but be painful, I know, but please take your time and tell me in your own words.'

'OK, Max, I will do my best. Perhaps it's best for me to start yesterday evening.'

Max Bellamy sat back in his chair and did what he had always been good at. He listened.

'I should perhaps begin by explaining that Ralph and I don't share the same bed anymore; in fact, we don't share the same room. There was a time when we couldn't keep our hands off each other for more than a few hours at a time; he is – he was – an attractive man, and there was never anything wrong with his appetite. But time passes, age marches on, and all that drastic and depressing age stuff creeps in. Ralph has always suffered to some extent with insomnia, partly because of that mind of his, which he finds very difficult to switch off. He also has a habit of having bright ideas in the middle of the night, which doesn't make sleep any easier either. We eventually agreed that it would be better and easier for both of us if we occupied different spaces, especially at night.'

She stopped suddenly, and Bellamy could see the cloud suddenly descend over her face, which paled even further than the drained look it had to begin with.

'And there's something else, Brigitte, is there?'

For a moment she hesitated, but then she seemed to resign herself.

'Ralph has never been the same since the disappearance of his youngest daughter, Chloe, over three years ago now. It wasn't just the way she disappeared, with weeks turning into months without any news whatever, it was the fact that she was, to use the English term, the apple of his eye – that wasn't just about her beauty, though she was beautiful – it was mostly about her being, as far as he was concerned, his true heir, or heiress, whichever you prefer.

'Ralph's eldest son and technically his heir, Miles, you have already encountered, and that is probably the right word with Miles; people do encounter him, and even in circumstances like this, Miles has to have his say. His mother was Ralph's first wife, and she was much the same sort of petty-minded, self-important windbag as Miles, to be honest, though I admit I am biased. I remember Mary saying to me on one occasion that she would always have a way of revenging herself on Ralph for what she saw as his desertion of her, and the way's name was Miles. Ralph's patient attempts to give the boy a proper education and interest him in the kind of science and technology that Ralph saw as important were doomed to failure from the start. Miles is a bureaucrat to his fingertips; he works for the family firm in that capacity, and yes, he does have some saving graces, in that he keeps everybody's feet on the ground, as he puts it, and places proper emphasis on the admin and the budgets. But he and Ralph are simply not on the same wavelength and were never going to be.'

'And I believe there was also a daughter from the same marriage?'

'Yes, you may have noticed her in the gathering earlier, though she would never seek to shove herself in your face as Miles does. Her name is Anne Atcliffe – Atcliffe is her married name – and though she is biologically Mary's daughter, she is in most other respects as much Ralph's daughter as Miles is Mary's son. The long, languid creature sitting next to her was her husband, Damien, an honest and considerate enough man, but perhaps not as much of this world as he would really need to be to take care of her fully. I think it would be fair to say that she has something of an inferiority complex in relation to both her father and her brother. She has never achieved the executive success of Miles, who is thorough and hard-working, even if totally unimaginative, and she's always been convinced that she's been a disappointment to her father, especially in comparison with her mercurial half-sister.'

Brigitte paused again, and this time Bellamy could see only too clearly the price she had had to pay to enter into a relationship with Manningham when the man already had one estranged wife and two children. The light flooding the room to her right showed her lined face in sharp relief, and Bellamy could see emotions represented there, though those of hatred and disgust were not amongst them. He felt it was almost certainly the case that, in spite of their rather separated existences, Brigitte did not hate her husband. If he was looking for some kind of double-bluff killer, making attempts to make the killing look like suicide which were so obvious and elementary that the real cause remained disguised, he very much doubted that it was Manningham's wife. He did personally like Brigitte Lacoste, and such feelings sometimes made him distrust his conclusions, but he could recognise that the reasons why he liked her – her bravery, her staying power, her intelligence – all made it more unlikely that she could ever have the personality of a killer.

Brigitte's silence continued, and Bellamy could see that something – perhaps a memory of Manningham, or a realisation about one of her family – was preoccupying her, and not pleasantly. But he knew he had to press on.

'Brigitte, if I thought it compatible with doing my job, I would say to you now, let's leave it there. But I do have to know the circumstances of last night and this morning. I cannot honestly say that I am at all convinced that this business was suicide—'

'Of course it wasn't suicide.' The abstracted expression faded suddenly. 'I didn't believe it this morning and I don't believe it now. Ralph could get very low at times, especially, as I said, after the experience of losing Chloe, but he was never the type to kill himself; he wasn't depressive, or alcoholic, or defeated. He could go into dark moods, and he could turn on people temperamentally, even me at times, though there was never a violent bone in his body, vicious as his tongue could be. And in any case, the whole thing was so ridiculously showy, with those damn pills spread all over the place – pills which, incidentally, looked to me like his beta blockers – and his study set up like something out of bloody Cluedo.'

'So, what do you think happened?'

'I don't know, Max. That's your business. But it wouldn't surprise me if he had a sudden heart attack. We knew he had angina, which is why he had those beta blockers.'

'But why should he, sitting quietly in his own home? And why would someone go to the trouble of trying to make it look like suicide, even if the attempt to do so was hopelessly inept?'

'I don't know, Max. Your business again.'

Blind alley number one. Max recognised the familiar feeling. Change tack and start again. A sudden beam of sun illuminated very clearly the anxiety and bewilderment on Brigitte's face. Back to the details.

'Did you see him last night, after you went to bed?'

'No, and what's probably more to the point, I didn't hear him either. He does sometimes keep late hours, but I don't generally sleep too well these days and I can hear him on the main corridor going to his room, or should I say rooms; he's practically got a large apartment to himself. You don't get to be a rich man and live in one poky room. But, of course, I didn't hear him at all last night.'

'When was the last time you saw him?'

'When we said goodnight. We may not co-habit as closely as we did, but we do still say goodnight to each other. I think it was just before nine o'clock; I'd decided to go to bed and read for a while. I was unsettled; I know it's nonsense to talk about omens and portends, but I just had a feeling that all was not well, that something was going to…'

The sentence was never finished. Bellamy turned his face away as he saw Brigitte slump forward on the sofa with her head in her hands, weeping quietly. He wondered if she had yet had a single opportunity to release her sorrow in the entire day so far.

Unlike many men, Bellamy didn't find overt grief embarrassing. He had seen it many times and in many circumstances, both in the course of his journalism and his police work, and he found its absence more awkward than its presence. People who had been recently bereaved could often be beset with all kinds of bureaucratic and circumstantial distractions, and many felt they were doing well and exercising the famous British stiff upper lip if they went for some time without letting their emotions go; Britons were still very suspicious of emotions, both their own and other people's. In his experience, suppression served only to make the eventual release all the more extreme.

Nor did he persuade himself that physical approaches, such as hugging her or kissing her lightly, were necessarily welcome; they might be, they might not, but in terms of heterosexual relationships, it was usually wise to prioritise caution.

Bellamy concentrated on making a few notes to summarise what he knew so far; it wasn't very much, but it was probably better than nothing. Manningham had died sometime between nine in the evening and eight in the morning, when the boy Paul found him. However, even that wasn't beyond dispute; he could have spoken to someone else in the night and the exact time of death had yet to be established.

He looked up from his notes and saw Brigitte was sitting upright, watching him with a curious expression somewhere between exasperation and admiration.

'I'm pleased to see you are keeping yourself occupied, Inspector,' she said, the ironic tone to her voice now very obvious.

Bellamy put his notes on the floor carefully and met her eyes.

'No doubt you think me a cold-blooded creature, Brigitte, but I have been close to the circumstances of death on many occasions, probably more than I care to remember, and I've deliberately contrived to avoid being eaten by cynicism; certain things need to happen, and everything becomes even more confused and misleading if they don't. I've known people making remarkably good efforts at simulating grief; on at least two occasions that I can remember, it was actually the murderer doing so. So, I'm quite practised now on knowing the difference between the genuine and the assumed, and in the presence of the genuine, I know it is healthier and more respectful to let it express itself. It's not difficult for anyone to admire a man like Ralph Manningham; we are all poorer for his loss, which makes me all the more resolved to get to the truth behind his death.'

For the first time that day, Brigitte smiled at him.

'Nicely put, Max. He didn't deserve this. I know it's faintly absurd to talk of justice in relation to the cold fact of death, but he had many more years of life and thought in him, and he's been through enough suffering to be due a lot of good times.'

'Yes, and now what can you tell me about Chloe? When did she disappear, and in what context?'

'The context, you'd have to say, was about her relationship with her father. Both of them were basically scientists; yes, Ralph was an industrialist, but for him, it was largely a way of putting his scientific brain into action. He had a genuine interest in trying to make life easier for people, and he had little patience with people, most notably his father, who didn't share his vision. He effectively elbowed his father out of the way and forced retirement on him. He schemed and plotted until he could command more of the shareholders of the company than his father could, and then they voted the old man out. John Manningham never quite recovered, and he was subsequently not averse to calling Ralph Judas to his face.

'Like many men's relationships with their fathers, the confrontation left a deep impression on Ralph, and when it became clear that Chloe was a highly able scientist, as well as being a girl with some considerable natural gifts for communication, Ralph saw the continuation of his family's progress in her. His relationship with his other two children, both of them with Mary Willows, was quite tense from the start, especially as Mary demanded a say and influence on them even after custody was awarded to Ralph and me. In spite of our best efforts, Mary managed to turn much of those kids' upbringing into a tug of war, and unfortunately it seems to have left indelible marks on Miles and Anne.

'Chloe was different from the start. Ralph wouldn't let Mary anywhere near her; neither would he agree to send her away to school, as Miles and Anne had been. Ralph educated her himself.'

From outside the room, Bellamy could hear a commotion going on at the front door. For a moment, he hovered between making a call to Elaine, then, with the sound of voices rising, he turned to Brigitte.

'Excuse me just for a moment or two, Brigitte; please don't go yet. I'll be as quick as I can.'

Anger, Bellamy generally found, was a weapon best used sparingly, or it lost all effectiveness, but on this occasion, he allowed his feelings to show.

'What in the HELL is going on?' he said, as he strode towards the main entrance. Elaine, he could see, was standing immediately in front of a man whose reddened face and aggressive stance suggested that he was trying to threaten or dominate her, not an easy task with Sergeant Price. He looked in late middle age, and though he bore a clear resemblance to Ralph Manningham, his whole foul-tempered and menacing demeanour contrasted sharply with Ralph Manningham's general cool and unflustered manner.

'And who the bloody hell might you be?' the man said, moving his whole body towards Bellamy as he spoke.

'I am Inspector Max Bellamy, and this is Sergeant Elaine Price, sir, and I strongly recommend you quieten both your tone and your threatening manner.'

The man deflated before his eyes and spent several seconds looking from Bellamy to Elaine in some bemusement.

'This lady did not tell me she was a police officer,' he said.

Bellamy's tone relaxed.

'Perhaps because you didn't give her the chance. May I ask who you are, and what you want here?'

'My name is Philip Manningham, and I am the younger brother of Ralph Manningham. I wish to see my brother's body and pay my last respects. He was an erstwhile traitor to my father and much too big for his boots on occasions, but he was my brother nevertheless and it is my right.'

'I'm afraid Mr. Manningham's body has already been sent for post-mortem, sir. The circumstances of the case made it imperative that an examination should take place as soon as possible. All proper procedures were observed. If you would care to join the other members of the family in the main living room, we will have a conversation shortly. I am sorry for your loss, sir, but you can at least be with your brother's family at this time.'

They were interrupted by a loud and scornful voice. Bellamy saw that Miles Manningham had emerged from the living room.

'Well, well, well! Uncle Philip appears on the scene, late as ever, trying to throw his weight around as usual.'

Bellamy's anger began to rise again and he turned to face the man.

'Please go back into the living room, Mr. Manningham, or I will arrest you for wasting police time.'

Miles tutted loudly, and for a moment their eyes met, but as Bellamy suspected, the other man's bark was very much more formidable than his bite, and within a few seconds only three people were left standing at the entrance, with a young constable hovering about twenty yards away in the unlikely event of Sergeant Price needing physical assistance.

'Well said, Inspector. I like to see a man who can take charge. I will go and tell young Miles where he gets off, and I dare say we will talk again soon.'

Bellamy smiled at Elaine and raised his eyes to the ceiling.

'Happy families, eh, Sergeant?'

'My sentiments exactly, sir.'

'I won't be very much longer with Ms. Lacoste, Elaine. I'll ask her to send the next one along. I'm going to want it to be Paul, the servant or whatever he is, because I think he had something to do with the media people coming here. I also think he may well sneak off, given half a chance, and that might mean us having something of a job to find him, so keep an eye on him, will you, or get a constable to do it?'

'Yes, sir.'

Brigitte Lacoste was sitting on the sofa with her head in her hands. For a moment, Bellamy thought further consolation would be needed before they could start again, but she raised her head and sat back wearily, watching him carefully as he returned to his chair.

'Your brother-in-law, Philip, has arrived, Brigitte,' Bellamy said.

'Oh, God, has he? Yes, I suppose someone must have tipped him off, with doubtless the most well-meaning intentions, but he doesn't make anything any easier, as you've no doubt just discovered.'

'He has already made a comment about Ralph's relationship with their father.'

Brigitte sighed and shook her head.

'Yes, well that doesn't surprise me, quite honestly, Max. I suppose most families with more than one sibling include a high-flyer and a no-hoper, but perhaps the distinction is not always as spectacularly obvious as it is with the Manninghams. Philip also inherited money from his father, though admittedly not as much as Ralph did, but Philip had spent his life up to that point fiddling about with various bits and pieces of retail, with one attempt at a newsagent business, one attempt at a menswear shop and so on, and he kept on fiddling about after his father's death, though with more money to waste. His main problem with Ralph was mostly that Ralph was successful.'

'You don't like him, do you?'

Brigitte smiled bleakly.

'No, I suppose that's pretty obvious. He can get so melodramatic about Ralph's so-called betrayal of their father; the old man was just about on his last legs, to be honest. Ralph knew his father was dying when he supposedly betrayed him; what he did, in fact, was give the old man a little peace before he died.'

'And did the old man see it like that?'

'Old Mr. Manningham became an expert in keeping his views to himself. He regarded business as another branch of politics, with every deal to be approached with careful and well-organised negotiation. Getting him to come out with a direct statement on what he thought of his son's style of management and general approach to business would have made getting blood out of a stone a mere walk in the park.'

'Even after his son had ousted him from the top job?'

'Especially after that. He knew Philip would make enough noise for the two of them. And he seemed to think, though he never said as much to me, that Ralph no longer had a role to play as his son; he was a businessman pure and simple. It wasn't one of those spectacular family bust-ups, it was a relationship that was never right in the first place and just faded away as a consequence.'

'OK.' Bellamy had a growing feeling that there was a crucial connection in the family somewhere which so far, he was missing. And, for all the intemperate Philip and the enigmatic Ralph, he suspected there was a crucial link to be made amongst the women.

'Let's just retrace our steps for a while, Brigitte, and look at Chloe, who doesn't fascinate me any the less for not actually being here. What you've said so far does seem to suggest that she was the apple of Ralph's eye, very much more so than her half-siblings.'

Brigitte looked up wearily, and Max made a mental note that he was going to need to move on to someone else quite soon.

'Yes, I think that's a fair statement, but you shouldn't get the impression that they were devoted to each other in a sloppy, sentimental kind of way. Ralph did a lot to home educate her from the start, and the emphatic way in which she responded to his encouragement showed him that he had a genuine heir, or heiress, whatever you want to call her. Chloe was our only child, Ralph and mine, and by the age of six, it was already obvious that she had a scientific brain to match his own. By the time she was in her late teens, she had already signed on for Ralph's Great Project.'

Something like an alarm bell suddenly sounded in Max's brain; it seemed as if a big hand had pointed emphatically in a certain direction. He'd had big-hand moments before, and they were sometimes pointing directly into a quagmire, but this one, he thought, was at least worth following up for the moment.

'What was Ralph's Great Project, and how was she implicated in it?'

'Ralph believed that the human species as a whole should be starting to look at sending pioneers to sites in space, and in particular, Mars and the Moon. He thought that, if we'd already got to the point where our own planet was beyond rescue, we should be thinking seriously about how and where we were going to carry on our story. Ralph was a rich man himself, of course, but he was in contact with some other guys – they were all men, as far as I can gather – who believed that the advances of AI should be used to mount a private expedition with many countries and peoples represented to colonise Mars and the Moon over the next century, while also adapting their environments to our needs. Ralph had already accepted that by the time the expedition left he would be too old and frail to be involved himself, but he thought Chloe could and should be one of the Mars pioneers.'

'And what did Chloe think?'

'Oh, she was all for it, or at least she was to start with. Then it became increasingly clear that doubts were setting in for her, and to make it all the more awkward, this was after he had effectively made her chief executive of the Manningham Corporation and said he would increasingly retire into the background and let her "get on with it", though letting her get on with it didn't stop him retaining the chairmanship of the board and pushing his own agenda; he thought he was being subtle about it, but Chloe clearly didn't. I think he was trying to avoid the painful family divides which he suffered with his father, and he thought, then, that she was entirely on the same wavelength as he was. But as far as Chloe was concerned, or as far as she was obviously starting to think, the emphasis should have been on using AI and other developing technologies to do what could be done to amend the damage which had already been done to our planet rather than turning our faces away to other places. The longer the arrangement went on with them dividing control of the corporation between them, the more fraught the situation became, until the day when Chloe had a real humdinger of a row with Dr. Yvonne Silowski, the Manningham head of research, who was pretty obviously in Ralph's camp. Silowski was so infuriated that she resigned.'

Max sighed. It was one of the moments he hated, when he had to ask a question of a vulnerable person at a particularly difficult time for them, but sometimes, there was nowhere else to go but ask the question.

'OK, Brigitte, and I know this is a bad time to ask, but what happened to Chloe?'

Brigitte gazed out of the window for so long that Bellamy began to suspect no answer would ever come, but eventually she spoke, in a voice full mostly of weariness and resignation.

'She simply disappeared. We waited and waited, we eventually started using private investigators, but no one seemed able to track down where she'd gone and what had happened to her. Day after day, week after week, and not a word, not even the ghost of a hint came back, even from some pretty well-established investigators.'

'That must have been incredibly difficult for both of you.'

'Yes.' The single word was the only one Brigitte was able to say, and for a moment, Bellamy thought she would break down again, but it seemed that one was all she was prepared to allow herself, and perhaps she had already exhausted herself with worry about her vanished daughter.

'Chloe comes across as a strongly self-willed character, from what you're saying.'

'Oh, yes, from an early age. She and Ralph were plotting plots and working out scenarios while she was still a child. The whole idea of using developed technology to practical effect, even in hostile environments, fascinated Chloe, perhaps even more so than her father's taste for space travel. As she grew up, she used to play in a substantial wooded area called Aitken's Wood – where the name comes from seems to be too far buried in history now for us to find out – which is part of the Manningham estate here. Ralph was particularly concerned to keep it as wild as possible in such a setting as the Houghton estate, for the purposes of research and investigation. Chloe would go there and stay in the area for days, sometimes on her own, sometimes with various friends. Teachers and parents would make stipulations about being able to visit and see what was going on, etc., and they went along with that, but kept most of their independence there, anyway. She was still going there, even more frequently on her own, not long before she went to university.'

'You must have had a good deal of anxiety about such trips.'

Brigitte sighed, and once again composed herself before replying.

'Yes, I did, especially when she went on her own. I asked Ralph to insist on someone going with her, but she seemed to have him under some kind of spell; whatever she wanted to do and whenever she wanted to do it was OK with Ralph once Chloe had wrapped him round her little finger with various idealistic but, to my mind, rather convoluted reasons. And believe me, Ralph is no pushover generally, for anyone except Chloe, which probably includes me.'

'OK, Brigitte, I'm going to get to the last question I intend to ask you, for the time being at least, and as you've probably guessed, it isn't an easy one in any circumstances either, but I have to ask it all the same. Do you believe that Chloe's death would have been enough for Ralph to take his own life, even three years later?'

'No, I don't. I don't believe he would ever do that on Chloe's account, even though he was devoted to her, because it would be so alien to the kind of relationship they had. And in any case, Ralph is – he was – a tough nut all the way down the line, and sooner or later, he would have got over it. My sense over recent weeks, and I don't believe anyone in the world, including Chloe, knows Ralph better than I do, was that his recovery process was well underway, when whatever happened today, happened.'

Brigitte flopped back in her chair and closed her eyes. Bellamy decided that enough was enough, for the time being at least.

'Brigitte, I anticipate that I'm going to be talking to everyone here for another two days, most probably. Please tell me if I'm wrong, but I suspect what you would like most at the moment is either to be on your own or to visit some particularly close friend somewhere.'

Brigitte sat up again and looked at the man before her with eyes registering a mixture of hope and anxiety.

'Well, yes, I would, but there are all sorts of things to do – the funeral to be arranged, all his friends and associates to be told—'

'The post-mortem will not be finished until tomorrow, and you could just as easily be talking to the funeral people in a friend's place not far away as you could here. However, it's your choice, of course. I'm not in the business of telling people how they should handle bereavements. Thank you for talking so frankly to me, and if you do decide to go somewhere for a few days, please let Sergeant Price know where you're going.'

Brigitte's head went down, and she sighed again, but a few moments later, she was up on her feet. She paused on her way to the door.

'Thank you, Max. I wish like hell none of this had ever happened, but since it has, I can't think of anyone else I'd rather have in charge of the aftermath. You don't really believe that he killed himself, do you?'

Max had experienced such a tactic before, and knew it as being particularly characteristic of politicians; the flattery followed by the big question, the feint and the strike.

'I don't believe the pills spilled on the table killed him, Brigitte. That, I'm afraid, is all I'm going to say at this stage. Please ask Elaine to send the young man Paul to me. Was he taken on after someone's recommendation?'

'He's the son of one of Ralph's business associates, who's a kind of media tycoon, if in a fairly limited way. He says he doesn't particularly like his father's type of work, and he would rather go into hospitality work, hotel and leisure management, that type of thing. He thought being a general dogsbody, as he calls it, might give him some inkling of what he's getting into, as well as providing him with a bit of pocket money. He's a decent lad who generally does as he's told, but he does have, I suppose I would have to say, a somewhat nosey disposition at times. It would perhaps be more charitably termed an inquisitive turn of mind.'

'May I know which business associate of Ralph's?'

'Christopher Shaw; he runs a programme-making production company.'

Click, click, click, thought Bellamy, remembering the beachside gambling machines of his youth. Sometimes they all fall into line just like that, and even look like they're going to before they do. He escorted Brigitte to the door.

'Thank you, Brigitte, and if you remember anything more, or you feel you need to talk to me, please don't hesitate to get in touch.'

For a moment, Bellamy considered what his talk with Brigitte amounted to. It would not have been unreasonable for her to have rejected his questioning altogether, or to have reacted to it in a more aggressive and resentful manner on the very day of her husband being found dead. Her control was remarkable, not only of herself but of the rest of the household. Emotional as she may be at the sudden death of her husband, she still talked and acted logically enough. He could read into that a certain indifference to her husband or interpret it as an example of her strength of mind. It did not take him long to decide on the latter. He could remember well enough his previous social and professional visits to the Manningham household, and he could also remember being not only impressed with Manningham himself, but also with the people he had around him, in the main. He concluded that he doubted very much whether there was anything of any great significance which Brigitte knew and hadn't told him, and neither was she protecting anyone who might be or have been intending to do harm to Ralph Manningham.

He spoke to Elaine.

'OK, can you send the lad to me, Elaine?'

Less than a minute later, a quick, brisk knock sounded on the door. Elaine's trademark, he thought. He opened it to reveal his sergeant beside a now rather apprehensive-looking young man, who was gazing from one face to the other, perhaps in the hope of extracting some clue to exactly where he stood with the police at this moment.

'Mr. Paul Shaw,' Elaine announced, with a quick grin as if to indicate that it wasn't her fault. Max stood aside and opened the door to let the young man enter the apartment. When he went in and closed it behind him, Shaw was looking more ill at ease than ever.

'Take a seat, Paul.'

Oddly enough, Paul Shaw chose to sit exactly where Brigitte had recently been sitting, and consequently, the light was generously illuminating his face. Max suspected that, in Brigitte's case, she didn't care, but in Paul's case, he didn't know. The boy's face had an odd kind of pallor rather unsuited to a healthy young man, which immediately alerted Bellamy to the fact that his interviewee had something he felt guilty about.

'Have you worked in this house for long, Paul?' Bellamy said evenly.

'About eighteen months now, a bit off and on with my studies and what have you.'

'Studies?'

'Yes, my dad feels that whatever business I'm going into, even if he doesn't much rate it, like hospitality, it needs to be known and experienced from brass tacks up, as he calls it.'

'Do you enjoy working here?'

'Oh, yes, well most of the time. Brigitte likes to be in control, and she can get a bit snappy at times if everything isn't, you know, absolutely ideal. She's a bit of a perfectionist.'

'Do you feel part of the household now?'

A flush had begun to appear on Shaw's face, turning it dappled red and white.

'Well, sort of. I'm really only a gofer, you know, do this, do that, sort of thing.'

Bellamy smiled.

'Perhaps so, Paul, but you're obviously quite a good gofer; Brigitte described you as something of a jack of all trades.'

The young man's attempt at a simper of modesty almost made Bellamy commit the unforgivable crime of laughing out loud.

'Well, I have to turn my hand to a variety of things here, it's true, but none of them are particularly difficult once you get the hang of them.'

'Why were you sent here, Paul?' Bellamy said suddenly.

'Sent here? What do you mean?' Suddenly, an expression of something like alarm showed on the young face.

Bellamy sat back and let him stew for a moment.

'I think it was you who let the media know about Mr. Manningham's death.'

Now alarm bells were visibly ringing in the young man's mind.

'Me? But why—'

'Because I think at least one of the reasons why you're here, and possibly the main reason, is to do your father's bidding and report back accurately on what's happening at Houghton Hall, who's saying what to whom, and what Mr. Manningham's current plans and projects amount to.'

'I'll talk to my father about it alright—'

'I would guess that you are the only person who regularly goes to every part of the house, and during the course of your duties, which I suspect are pretty light most of the time, you would have plenty of opportunities to pass the word on to a media connection, probably one connected with your father's work. No one else in the house talks to the media, as far as I can see – they would be more likely to seek to keep away from them. The local police were summoned when Mrs. Manningham informed the authorities, at the same time as she spoke to a senior politician. I can see no one else in any part of the proceedings who would be likely to have informed the media.'

'It's no crime, to keep my father informed—'

'I didn't say it was, though I suspect Mrs. Manningham might well see your communication with the media as a betrayal of her trust. What do you think?'

'I don't see why – they would have found out soon enough. This is a rural community; they would be bound to pass information around—'

'But this morning, they didn't need to, Paul, did they? You'd done it for them. You told someone from your father's production company, who no doubt has many other contacts in both the written and broadcasting media, and it's my belief that you were sent here by your father largely to do just that.'

Bellamy let the silence fall and stay for a moment, like a shadow over the conversation. Shaw was now very near to tears.

'You're not going to tell Brigitte – I mean, Mrs. Manningham, are you?'

'I think Mrs. Manningham probably worked it out some time ago, Paul.'

Bellamy had concluded that both Brigitte and Ralph Manningham himself must have known what Paul and his father were up to. Manningham, with his eccentric genius reputation and his spectacular expeditionary plans, was probably not entirely averse to the idea of the extent of his big plans finding its way into the media, and playing cat and mouse with young Paul might have amused him; he might even have been genuinely wanting to give him a leg up in his chosen profession. The family had probably known Paul since babyhood. Yet one more example of the use of the young by their elders, ostensibly to benefit the young but mainly to suit the needs of the old. Bellamy wondered how many menial tasks Paul Shaw would have been called upon to perform over the months to justify his placement in the Manningham home, and what occasional titbits he had sometimes been fed to keep his devious father happy.

'Do you really think so?'

Paul Shaw's now distinctly agitated tone brought Bellamy back to the reality of the figure now slumped before him.

'Probably, Paul, but if you want to stay in her good books, as I think you probably are most of the time – she has said to me how useful you have been in the house – I think you really should tell me everything you know. When did you first contact your father?'

'Oh, God, I don't speak directly to Dad. I'm not important enough to have immediate access to that particular ear. No, I speak to a guy who is only a little way further up the gofer scale than I am, and I'm not going to tell you his name, even if you put electrodes on my balls or something.'

Good God, Bellamy thought to himself, the boy is still living in animated fantasy world.

Shaw hurried on.

'Sorry – did I say that out loud? You've got me a bit flustered. Anyway, I heard you saying to the media guys that you used to be a journo yourself, Mr. Bellamy, so you must understand that I'm not going to name names.'

'Journalistic sources are a bit different from guys you occasionally whisper things to, Paul. However, I'm not much interested in the guy's name, anyway. What I am interested in is when and how you found out that Mr. Manningham was dead.'

'I saw Mrs. Manningham come out of Mr. Manningham's study this morning, and then I heard her making her phone calls, then I saw Mr. Manningham slumped at his desk in the study. And, yes, since you know it all now anyway, it was something obviously important enough for me to report in, as my father calls it, even though the dumbo I am supposed to talk to started off not believing me. "Listen," I said, "you can believe what you like, but when everyone else has got this story before us, my dad will be coming for you or me, and I will be able to prove that I made this call. So sort that one out, pal".'

'So you "reported in" on Mr. Manningham's death, did you? What else did you report in, Paul? Details of Mr. Manningham's projects? The things which happened between Mr. Manningham and his relatives, including his wife? Just how far did the spying go, Paul, because spying is what we're talking about, isn't it?'

For a few moments, the two men were eye to eye, and the tone of Bellamy's voice made clear enough what he was implying. The younger man's face had reddened again, and suddenly tears really did begin to appear in his eyes.

'I know what it must look like to you, Mr. Bellamy, but I'm not a spy. Whatever my father wants me to do, or whatever his real reasons were for sending me here, I respect Mr. and Mrs. Manningham and the main reason I work here, as far as I'm concerned, is not just to get used to the general domestic stuff but to let something of what they are rub off onto me. I'm not sneaking any big, bad secrets away from them to tell my dad, one because they haven't got any big, bad secrets, as far as I know, and secondly because they're both much cleverer than I am, and they wouldn't let me know if they had.'

The boy is not that good an actor, Bellamy thought; *he's telling me what he really believes. What his father's version would be of the reasons why he was sent into the Manningham household might be different, but if there is evil intent here, it is probably the father's.* It was a long shot, Bellamy reflected, the idea that this boy was a lot more subtle than he seemed and Manningham had some imbroglios, sexual or professional, which were near enough to coming out to give him suicidal tendencies. But, like the theory that Brigitte Lacoste had tired of her husband to the extent that she wanted to dispose of him, it just wouldn't wash. *Back to the drawing board*, Bellamy thought wearily. *But at least the human beings here are holding themselves a little above the lowest common denominator.*

In the meantime, this young man is obviously desperately worried that this is all going to land on his father's desk, with the implication that he has been exceeding his brief. Bellamy's inbuilt affection for the young and vulnerable asserted itself.

'OK, Paul, thanks for that, and for talking honestly to me. I am not planning to talk to your father at this stage, but if I do, I will say that in my opinion you are doing the best you can with a not very easy brief. But I must urge you not to talk to any of the media people out there about what you know or don't know; it would be much better for the moment if you kept yourself to yourself, within the house as much as is possible, at least until this case is finally resolved.'

The boy's relief was almost embarrassing.

'Yes, certainly, Mr. Bellamy. Whatever you say, sir. Is that it now?'

Bellamy nodded and found himself alone again in a matter of seconds. His face took on an expression which those familiar to him would have recognised, a kind of straight-mouthed sulk which said that he was about to do something which he anticipated might be particularly difficult in one way or another. He picked up his phone and called Elaine.

'Hi. Is everything OK where you are? The media behaving themselves?'

'No. When do the media ever behave themselves? We've had two so far trying to sneak out of our orbit and get in at the back of the house. I've told the rest of them I'll empty the place altogether if I find anyone else trying it on. Who's next up, sir?'

'I'm going to speak to Miles Manningham. I've been wondering whether I should leave it until tomorrow, but I'd just as soon get it over with. He'll be the last one today, and then we'll establish if anyone has any intention of leaving tomorrow. Send him along, Elaine, please, and when I've done with him, could we have a word?'

'Yes, sir. Good luck.'

About two minutes later, a solid knock announced the arrival of Miles Manningham. Bellamy sighed almost inaudibly to himself and then went to open the door.

'Mr. Manningham,' he said with a game attempt at a smile.

'The very same,' Manningham said as he breezed into the apartment. 'Although it might make sense to call me Miles, so as not to confuse me with the old man.'

As Bellamy anticipated, an attempt by the man to set the agenda right from the start.

Bellamy managed to sigh internally again. The succession of largely infantile attempts to rule the roost which seemed to be approaching induced both a physical and mental sense of weariness in him.

'Very well, Miles, if that is your wish. Please take a seat.'

Manningham sat himself down exactly where Bellamy had been sitting for the last two interviews. Bellamy responded by pulling a wooden chair from the wall and sitting on it, at a forty-five-degree angle to his interviewee; even without the bright light from the window, he could see Manningham mostly in profile and profiles were always revealing.

'Did you get on well with your father, Miles?'

The interviewee's exasperation showed clearly in his reply.

'You don't mess about, do you, Mr. Policeman? Straight for the jugular. Take the oldest son, and if everyone knows he doesn't hit it off too easily with the old man, there you have a ready-made suspect. I'm quite disappointed, Inspector. I thought you might have more originality, since you've been a pressman yourself.'

'One or two of my colleagues have told me that your business is not as secure these days as it has been at times in the past, Mr. Manningham. Would you have any comment to make on that?'

'Insinuations. Bloody insinuations. It's as if I'm fair game now the old man has died. Firstly, you imply that I might have hated the man, then we're on the tack of me being desperate for money to keep my business afloat.'

Manningham was looking at him with daggers in his eyes, but Bellamy was entirely used to hostility, and he did not react. He knew more was coming and he simply determined to stay silent until it did.

'I didn't hate him. I had reason to hate him, without a doubt; he ditched my mother when he had no further time for her and he was always more concerned with his various fancy ideas than he was with being a husband and father. But I recognised years ago that the two of us were just essentially not compatible, just as he and my mother were not compatible. Once I put that barrier up between us, it got easier. I didn't wish him any harm; I just didn't want him in my life, and I kept him out of it most of the time.'

'And is that how your wife saw it?'

For some seconds, Manningham simply sat and glared. Bellamy had the distinct impression that, had he been a Manningham employee, this is the point when he would have been given his cards. It was clearly getting through to the man that he was now dealing with someone who could not be intimidated and was not afraid to ask awkward questions.

'No, I suppose I'd have to say that it wasn't. But it's a hell of a jump, Inspector, to go from a little domestic difference of opinion to any kind of a conspiracy against an old man—'

Bellamy made an instantaneous decision to "float a boat".

'Have you ever struck your wife, Mr. Manningham?'

Another aggressive pause, and on this occasion, Bellamy did have the impression that the other man might have been violent towards him if he thought he could get away with it.

'What the hell do you mean? How dare you? What has she said?'

Bellamy leaned forward towards his interviewee.

'It's a perfectly simply question, Manningham. You come across to me as a man not entirely in control of his emotions and how they relate to his actions. When we are looking into a case where a man has suddenly died, men like you are inevitably going to be under suspicion. I think it quite likely that you might well reach the point where violence could become a possibility.'

'My father killed himself. As everyone knows. You are just seeking to justify your existence. This should all be over now; everyone should be heading home to grieve in their own way…'

'The exact manner of your father's death has not yet been established, Mr. Manningham, either by me or the coroner. Have you struck your wife?'

Now Manningham was on his feet and, once again, Bellamy had the impression that, were it not for his police credentials, violence would not be far away.

'What the hell right have you got to ask me that?'

Bellamy used one of the weapons he had developed in his armoury over the years, helped, as he knew very well, by his blue eyes and the bland neutrality his face could adopt. It was a simple stare, which he knew served to have a calming and reducing effect on those he was dealing with from journalistic days onwards, and especially those whose consciences were not clear.

He did not rise from his own chair.

'Mr. Manningham, I am investigating a man's death. If someone known to have a capacity for violence was in the vicinity of the deceased at the time of death, I have every right, as the investigating officer, to establish the extent of his capacity for violence so that I can then make some realistic estimate of whether or not he was involved in the death. Your attitude to your wife, and hers to you, suggests to me the possibility of violence in the relationship. You know well enough that I will also be speaking to your wife. Will she have anything to say to me?'

Manningham had paled now and was slowly resuming his seat. Bellamy's stare remained unbroken.

'There was an accident,' Miles Manningham said slowly, his voice having dropped. 'In fact, there have been two accidents.

On one occasion, something I was holding did accidentally make contact with my wife, who had approached me on my blind side; she alleged the action was deliberate, but I denied it then and I deny it now. On another occasion, I swung my arm aggressively, thinking she had moved from where she was, and she hadn't, so yes, I did strike her, but by accident. If such things constitute a "capacity for violence", Inspector, then I suppose I have it, but the idea that I would raise a finger to my father, who never touched me in anger in all the time I knew him, is absurd. Are you satisfied now? Do you intend to pursue this line of questioning, or can we move to something more sensible?'

'I hear your view of the incidents, Mr. Manningham. I suspect your wife's might be a rather different interpretation. But we will move on, by all means; whether or not you will regard the move as more sensible is up to you. The elephant in the room at the moment continues to be your half-sister, Chloe. Perhaps you could tell me something about her.'

Miles Manningham seemed momentarily to deflate. Even the mention of his half-sister produced a clear reaction in him; he sat down, and when he spoke again, his anger had been replaced with a sudden sadness.

'Chloe was rather special. To lose her in such a mysterious and even now unexplained way was, I think, more than the old man could deal with. Chloe and my father were like soul partners; they saw the world in the same kind of way, they perceived it as being in the same kind of crisis situation, and they thought similarly about how best to respond to the crisis – or, at least, initially they thought similarly about it.'

'Your half-sister was lost about three years ago, wasn't she?'

'Yes, it must be about that by now, though I find it difficult to think of it in those terms; I find it difficult, to be honest, to think of her as "gone" or, even worse, "dead" at all.'

This was so much a different Miles Manningham that Bellamy

couldn't help wondering whether he was dealing with a Jekyll and Hyde type of character.

'You were obviously fond of your half-sister, Miles,' he said gently.

'Yes – well, most of the time. Chloe had the kind of smile and manner that could melt any male heart, even those of siblings. By rights, I should have grown to hate her; she was much cleverer than me, my father worshipped the ground she walked on, whereas he hardly noticed me at all most of the time. But Chloe had a way of making anyone she spoke to think they were the greatest creature in the world. My father thought he saw in her the way of making his dreams and ambitions come true, even after he no longer had the strength to physically pursue them himself.'

'What were his dreams and ambitions?'

Manningham's glance returned to its former suspicion.

'I would have thought, in all the time you were talking to Brigitte, that would have become abundantly clear.'

'Different people have different interpretations, Miles; that is what an investigation is all about. How would you describe your father's dreams and ambitions?'

'Unworldly, would be the word, I suppose. A good word, at that, both literally and metaphorically. He thought the cause of Earth was pretty much lost and it behove the species to invest in an elite team to adapt the atmosphere of the Moon and Mars – well, the Moon to begin with – and make them colonies of Earth, to eventually become the new homes of the species. Chloe, he considered, was an ideal candidate, not only to be one of the colonisers but one of the leaders. The two of them would sometimes talk for hours about both the economies and practicalities of establishing the space colonies and making them viable, as opposed to concentrating the efforts on staying on Earth to do whatever might be possible to improve matters.'

'Did Chloe really share her father's enthusiasm for these space projects, or was she more concerned about prioritising the existing demands of the planet?'

'A good question, and the nearest I can get to answering it is to say that they did argue, and when they argued, it was almost invariably about the means rather than the ends. Chloe was interested in the new start on space colonies project in theory, but in practice, she generally considered that our existing planet should be prioritised, that the technologies available should be used to alleviate, as much as possible, the existing problems on Earth before new worlds were set up and colonised. We all thought, in the early stages, that the two of them were largely on the same page, after the endless conversations they used to have about ends and means and the wherewithal to do what needed to be done. But as time went on, their differing positions became more entrenched. My father eventually thought that making Chloe chief executive of the company would enable her to further her own objectives and interests, while he, as chairman, could pursue the research side. I suppose he'd decided they could just agree to differ, though it became increasingly obvious that Chloe wasn't going to think like that. It put a lot of pressure on both of them.'

'So they were beginning to go their separate ways when Chloe disappeared?'

'Yes, they were. Her complete disappearance bemused and shocked everyone, and after a time, even my father had to accept that she was lost. Though whether he ever did really accept it, who can say? He was not the man to accept what he didn't want to accept, however much evidence there was contradicting him, as is shown in his refusal to recognise that he and Chloe were taking the business in opposing directions.'

Bellamy considered whether to challenge this but decided against it. In the last analysis, it was the realities he was concerned with, not Miles Manningham's interpretation of them. It seemed a suitable time to begin winding up their conversation, but Manningham still had some more to offer. Perhaps the exposure of his violent tendencies towards his wife was making him feel vulnerable.

'Chloe had her own secret place to go, you know, when she was a kid, and at various times ever since.'

'Are you talking about Aitken's Wood?'

'Yes, I am. You are one step in front of me, Inspector. How do you manage to know about Aitken's Wood?'

Now he is trying to bond, Bellamy thought, *all chaps-together stuff, to try and put his violence towards his wife out of my mind. Why do they think that these simple and predictable manoeuvres are enough to deflect me?*

'I spent some time talking to your stepmother. What can you tell me about Aitken's Wood?'

'Well, Chloe, who was very impressionable about these things, you know, in the way girls tend to be, saw it as the nearest she could get round here to a proper wilderness. She would sometimes go there and stay there for days, which really alarmed my father. Even allowing for the fact that Aitken's Wood was part of the Manningham estate and behind the estate barriers, Chloe was still a young girl, camping on her own. Dad insisted that she find a female friend to stay with her, and she would sometimes say she had, though I knew for a fact that the friend who was supposed to be female was sometimes male, though she didn't tell Dad about it and no one dared sneak on her. She could be a real handful when what she'd decided to do was challenged, could Chloe. I doubt whether anything particularly sexual ever happened, all the same; if it did, it wouldn't have been anything likely to make her pregnant. Chloe was not exactly a tomboy, but—'

'Go on. But what?'

'Well, she was easy with boys, but more in a kind of matey way, and only with a certain kind of boy – not necessarily gay, though I'd guess one or two of them were, but unchallenging in the sexual sense, if you see what I mean. The ones just interested in getting their ends away – pardon me, but you know what I mean – she saw through very easily. The scientifically minded, gay or otherwise, tended to be her male friends, and even they didn't get any closer than she wanted them to, which wasn't very.'

'Did you think Chloe was gay herself?'

'Oh, Lord, I wouldn't know. I'm no kind of judge of these things. Are you?'

Bellamy decided that this question could safely be ignored, and he also recognised, with a certain pang of gratitude, that he had probably talked to this man for as long as he needed to. Miles Manningham was an angry man on one level, probably stemming from what he saw as his failures and inadequacies, and he was undoubtedly a man given to occasional and possibly criminal violence, primarily in the direction of his wife. As Bellamy had every intention of speaking to Mrs. Manningham, that was a subject he would need to return to, because Manningham's sanitised version of incidents when he had directed violence at his wife sounded like only half the story, and Bellamy was not the man to let one crime go unrecognised in the pursuit of another.

Bellamy arranged his papers and stood up, making his intentions all too clear. Manningham stood up himself and paused uncertainly.

'I assume you're going to be talking to my wife?' he said quietly. A lot of fight seemed to have gone out of him.

'Yes, I will be,' Bellamy said.

'So, just after losing my father, the chances are I will be losing my wife,' Manningham said, halfway to the door.

Bellamy used the eyes for a moment before answering.

'I have known a number of men who have been overtly violent towards their wives, and I've been involved in the prosecutions of a few. What they all seem to have in common is a tendency to see the problem as someone else's, as if unreasonably visited on them by an unknown hand. The future of your marriage, Mr. Manningham, is entirely in the hands of you and your wife, as it has always been. In the longer term, nothing said to me is going to make an iota of difference. It's my belief that women are generally too tolerant in this respect, but how Mrs. Manningham thinks and acts is the province of Mrs. Manningham alone, and I have no intention of attempting to make it otherwise. Thank you, Mr. Manningham, and I would appreciate it if you could ask my sergeant to come and see me now. Please ensure that you do not leave the house permanently until my investigation is finished; I don't doubt Brigitte will be prepared to extend her hospitality.'

Manningham shut the door with almost a bang. Once again, Bellamy thought, he is only just in charge of his temper. A few minutes later, a familiar knock sounded, and Bellamy turned away from his notes to see Elaine standing over him.

'Enough for one day, Elaine, I think. I'm going to look in detail at these notes and then think about the whole business as dispassionately as possible. Has anyone stated any intention of leaving the house permanently?'

'No, sir. The uncle is not exactly being welcomed with open arms, but Ms. Lacoste is willing to put him up for a night or two in the circumstances. Are you going home, sir?'

'Yes, I am. I need the peaceful atmosphere of my own HQ to get my head straight with this one. I would expect Colin Thurston to contact me there, if he thinks he's got anything of interest. As pathologists go, he's generally generous with his information, unlike some of them when it's like getting blood out of a stone.'

'What about security here, sir?'

'Well, we need a couple of people overnight, I think. No one's going to grumble about staffing costs on this one; they want it settled quietly and as soon as possible. But we can leave that to the locals, I think, Elaine. If you could just go and check that that's been attended to, I'll join you at the car. In the meantime, I'll give those hacks at the front of the place another warning, just to be on the safe side.'

Eventually, and gratefully, Bellamy reached the peaceful surroundings of his own home. On this occasion, Louise was spending the evening with him; her work called her away on various conference and media demands, so a quiet night in was not too common an occurrence. In the course of their working days, they both tended to spend a lot of their time talking or listening, and to spend a few companionable hours in silence together was a pleasant relaxation.

Louise could tell when her husband was thinking about something connected with work, and this could sometimes put him in the awkward situation of not being able to discuss the issues with her even when he wanted to. Sometimes, the same thing applied in reverse. Louise had to dabble in politics at times, when political decisions had ramifications which connected with her environmental interests, and politicians could be very jumpy about their words being discussed; many of them spent a lot of their time trying not to have anything even vaguely controversial attributed to them.

She knew that if Max really wanted to brood alone, he would retreat to his study cum library; for as long as he was in the living room with her, he was either enjoying the silence or waiting for a suitable moment to say what was on his mind. If he ever touched on any cases he was concerned with, he could only ever talk in generalities, but sometimes the generalities could be very relevant to the gist of the case.

He was sitting in a kind of sprawl on the sofa, his head back and his eyes occasionally closing. *It's like waiting for him to lay an egg*, she thought. She sometimes amused herself by making her own estimations about when he would actually come out with whatever he was going to say, as if betting on a countdown. Eventually, he opened his eyes and looked across at her.

'Did you ever hear of something called the Judas gene?'

The trick, Louise said internally, was to not be surprised.

'No, I can't say I have. Is it genetic or psychological?'

'Oh, strictly speaking, the latter, I suppose. It was an old editor of mine who first came out with it. Ed Mowbray, his name was; he could be an odd combination of cynic and sentimentalist at times. He taught me a lot about interview techniques. He believed that to do it effectively, you really needed to get a grasp on people's motivations, because the conventional sets of motives – money, power, revenge, etc. – were often not the real story, or not the whole story, anyway. "Some people," he said, "odd as it might seem, appear to act as if they have a kind of built-in and unavoidable urge to betray someone close to them. Even though they might realise how incredibly risky it is, and even when it directly contradicts everything else that they consider themselves to stand for, they can still do it, as if driven by an inner compulsion they can't do anything about".'

'Interesting. In fact, I could think of a few examples without having to think too hard.'

'Yes, so can I. It's like a kind of fatalism, and the other thing he said he'd noticed about it was the generational thing, hence the "gene". Those who do it are often repeating something which their parents or grandparents did, if not in exactly the same form. In the case I'm thinking about – no names, Lou, but then you know that – the guy betrayed his father down the line; he shoved him out of the company which the old man had actually created, took over the thing himself and completely changed it, pointing it in a whole new direction. And it seemed that his old man had done much the same kind of thing to his old man. So, when I seek to understand the motives of a brilliant daughter of this family, I can't help thinking about old Mowbray and his Judas gene notion.'

At this point, Bellamy's phone made its presence felt. Probably just as well, Louise thought, bearing in mind that she had known

Ralph Manningham, and she knew something of his background. Max would shortly remember that, and then the conversation might start to get strained.

When he heard whose voice it was on the other end, Bellamy took the phone into his study. Conversations with pathologists always did have to be confidential.

'Hello, Colin. What have you got for me?'

'You're no small-talker, are you, Bellamy? Time is money and all that, I suppose. How are you, Colin? Oh, not so bad, Max, how are you?'

'Sorry. I've been brooding on the case I think you're about to tell me something about.'

'Yes, you do brood, Bellamy, I've noticed that. Well, brood on this. Your guy Manningham died of natural causes; a coronary, in fact. Rather surprising, given the medication regime he was on, though how good he was at observing it, I don't know. The pills on his desk, spilled or not, were straightforward atenolol beta blockers, and he would have known perfectly well that they wouldn't kill him, even in numbers. And Tom Hollins knows the details now; he's been practically breathing down my neck. Do we have powers that be sniffing around here, Max?'

'Yes, I'm afraid we do. They get heavy with him, and now he knows that he's probably going to get heavy with me. He'll want me to wrap it up, then he can get them off his back.'

'You don't sound as if you want to wrap it up, Max. Don't you believe in a quiet life?'

'As and when it's possible. Here, I don't think it is. Not yet anyway.'

'Don't look gift horses in the mouth, Max, one of the first lessons for a reasonably peaceful life. You're off the hook; it's a straightforward medical case. The guy even had a history of heart disease. Give yourself a break; close the folder and move on.'

'Comments noted, Dr. Thurston. And let me tell you that

while I might wish deep down that the thing was all over, some little so and so is whispering in my ear that it isn't.'

When he finished his call with Colin Thurston, Bellamy put his phone down on the table in front of him and started counting. *It will go again before I get to fifty, and it will be Tom Hollins. Do I want it that way? No. Will it be that—*

His phone sounded on number thirty-six.

'Hi, Inspector Max. Tom Hollins. You heard the news?'

'Yes. Colin Thurston's just phoned me.'

'Well, you can't lead that raid of yours as that's done now, with somewhat so-so results. I'll come back to that; we could maybe think of a different approach next time around. As it is, the Manningham case is about done and dusted, if it was ever a case in the first place.'

Bellamy had become very expert at long inner sighs which didn't interrupt the flow of conversation when there was such a flow to interrupt, but on this occasion, Hollins had been so predictably disappointing that he found the sigh difficult to conceal. He followed it with a deep breath, and charged in.

'Ralph Manningham was not stupid enough to believe that taking multiple beta blockers would either rescue him if he was having a heart attack or kill him if he was attempting suicide. Neither was he the type to leave stuff like that lying around. Someone made an admittedly crude attempt to paint the scene as a suicide; that is a crime. Or someone scared him or threatened him enough to cause him to have a heart attack; that's also a crime. There was also evidence of something heavy, such as a body, being dragged from the patio outside Manningham's study into his study. Moving a dead body without authorisation is also a crime. Failing to do anything to help someone who's in the throes of a heart attack is also a crime, in certain circumstances. Need I go on?'

His words were followed by a heavy pause, and Max knew he had once again trod on an old friend's toes, except that these days the old friend was a superior police officer. He was rehearsing something to say to change the tone when Hollins replied.

'I know that voice of yours, Max; it's the one that says "I'm in this up to the eyeballs and I'm going to do it my way or I'm not going to do it at all". Can't you let the local bobbies in that area clean it all up?'

This time, Max thought, think a bit longer before you speak.

'I'm sorry, Tom, that's not what I was trying to put across. I am sort of local to it anyway; I'm in the same county, when all's said and done. But I haven't forgotten who's looking on in the wings at this case. I got the impression from you that Gregson was anxious about yanking the politicians' chains if and when something came out about Manningham, the Tory Party donor, having something in his past or present which might embarrass the knobs who don't want to be embarrassed. The fact that Manningham's death was a natural coronary doesn't actually mean that there isn't some kind of skeleton in the cupboard. If I was still a hack, any editor worth his or her salt would be saying to me, "don't leave the story half-written. We want it all, before some opportunist rag puts its hands into its deep pockets and finds out the whole truth before we do, making us look like a lot of plonkers".'

'What – you still think there might be something in Manningham's background?'

'I think it's a possibility. A guy who's on regular heart medication and is generally seen as taking reasonable care of himself suddenly has a heart attack, sitting in his own study in his own home of a quiet evening. Was someone putting the squeeze on him about something? Was some disreputable old habit coming home to roost? Had he offended someone badly in the past – he was a powerful man who no doubt got up some people's noses on the way up, as powerful men always do – or was he threatening to reveal something which the party hierarchy didn't want him to reveal, meaning they were putting on him the kind of pressure which gives people heart attacks?'

To his surprise, he could make out the sound of Hollins chuckling.

'You bewilder me as ever, Max. You can sit there one minute like a dumb mute, as inscrutable as you like, and the next you're talking nineteen to the dozen, all that remorseless logic directed at being a crusader without an identifiable enemy.'

Hollins's voice changed in mid-stream to a different, harsher tone.

'Don't tell me you want to carry on the investigation for the sake of politicians, Max, because that's just a bit too much for me to swallow.'

'No, no, Tom, you miss the point. I want to carry it on in spite of politicians. They don't want me to find the truth, they want me to find a version of it they can live with, and if it's not what they call good news, they want to get their hands on it before anyone else does. Yes, they'll happily accept that a guy who was known to have heart problems just suddenly dropped dead – overwork, not taking care of himself as much as he should, etc. – all easily assimilated, just one of those things, end of story. But this one just isn't as simple as that, and there are still issues to it, issues which could be important.'

Now the silence was Hollins thinking. One of the reasons, Max thought, why Hollins was the kind of policeman he could work with; he was a thinker.

'Alright, let's give it another three days maximum. You'll have to square it with Brigitte, of course; she will sure as hell know now that Ralph died of a heart attack, and if that's that, as far as she's concerned, you could have problems continuing an investigation in her house. But that's not my problem, it's yours. Mine's Gregson. I've probably got the better part of that deal, Max. Keep me posted.'

There it is again, Max thought, as he put down the phone. However careful, however meticulous his consideration, there was always one angle which he didn't allow for, or which he didn't give as much weight to as he should.

Brigitte Lacoste, the woman who stood out from the rest of her family like a giant among pygmies, in Bellamy's opinion; where would he be, and where would the investigation be, if she took the same line as Hollins? And if Hollins, who was an outstanding and thoughtful policeman, thought like that, it was surely not too difficult to imagine Brigitte taking the same line. He was operating in Brigitte's house, and the nature of the investigation made it difficult for it to be successfully continued anywhere else. If Brigitte had also now concluded that the investigation was over, continuing it could become very difficult, and even more so if she decided to get in touch with her exalted political friends.

Back in the living room, Louise could see clearly enough that her husband was preoccupied and worried. She usually felt it better not to try and interfere with his cases, but she knew both of the Manninghams rather better than he did, and for once, she felt it was at least worth seeing if she could help.

'You look positively careworn, Max. I wouldn't normally ask what you're careworn about, but if it's the Manningham case, I do at least have some knowledge of them; quite a lot, in Brigitte's case. Is there anything I can contribute?'

Bellamy turned towards her, and she could see in his eyes, which to her could sometimes – but only sometimes – be accurate meters of his state of mind, the kind of wrestling with ambiguity which could tax him, philosophical as he generally was towards his job.

Policing, like journalism, had to have room for improvisation, he thought, and sometimes the course of action to which you felt naturally drawn was not necessarily the wrong one.

'Tom Hollins thinks that, because we know now that Ralph Manningham died from a heart attack, there probably isn't much more to investigate and I should give the whole thing over to the local plods. I've talked quickly enough to get some more time from him, but if Brigitte Lacoste decides along the same lines, it's going to be pretty difficult to continue the investigation in her house, and even more difficult to continue it outside of her house. You know Brigitte better than I do. Would you care to predict what she will think? If you wouldn't, Louise, please say so; I'm looking for handholds here, I know, but that doesn't oblige you to provide them.'

'Brigitte is not one for unfinished business in her professional life, Max; it's not always possible, in her work or mine, to cross all the t's and dot all the i's, but she will seek to get as close to it as she can. When it comes to the death of her husband, to whom she was and is devoted, she won't want to call a halt until everything is well sorted to her satisfaction. Even if Ralph did die of a natural heart attack, and I see no reason to disbelieve the doctor in that respect, it's still a death in suspicious circumstances, and I think she will see it like that. Yes, Ralph had heart trouble, but he was taking medication for it, and she's said to me that he was very conscientious about taking it. He was in his own study on a quiet evening; we know of no disturbance, no break-in, no family row, no bad news just received. Yes, it could be that his heart just ran out of time, but from Brigitte's point of view, she's lost the guy she loved more than anyone else in the world to a sudden and largely inexplicable heart attack. She has to now face the rest of her life without him and no doubt she will, but she will most definitely want to know exactly why she has to.'

The next day, his wife's words were still resounding in Bellamy's mind in the car on the way to Houghton Hall, and Elaine had to repeat herself before she managed to get his full attention.

'What?' he said, as the words penetrated through his morning dullness. 'What kind of fracas at the hall?'

'Well, the local force were on to me about the media, who were up to all kinds of stuff in the late afternoon and overnight, apparently.'

'To you?'

'Yes, sir. They got it through their heads that the media around the hall was my department.'

'Oh, right. No, they didn't, Elaine. They're just trying it on. I'll make the position as clear as crystal when we get there.'

'OK, sir, though the locals decided, and I agreed with them, to keep all the journos outside the hall gates. Brigitte has even got a dog patrol organised after she saw one of them blatantly looking in through the windows on the southern side of the hall, the other side of the main gates. There was also some kind of row going on between the people in the hall; apparently, two of the Manninghams, Miles and Rachel, decided "investigation over, we're off home now".'

'And Brigitte stopped them?'

'Apparently so, sir, and they're not going to mess with Brigitte, especially since they don't yet know what was in the will.'

'I hope he left everything to Brigitte. He is – or was – much too clever a guy to divide up his money and watch them at each other's throats about it.'

Bellamy didn't care to tempt fortune by depending on that; he had form with the chaos that could be caused in families by wills, sometimes by people generally considered safe and sensible individuals, and he'd already seen the nature of some members of the Manningham family. However, that, fortunately, was unlikely to be his business in this case. He wanted to be on best form, as much as possible, before re-entering the hall and resuming the investigation.

The feeling returned to him again, a feeling much more characteristic of his journalism days than his police career. His hack instincts had always been much vaguer, and therefore the directions they pointed out to him were probably more likely to be unreliable, but every now and then, and usually on matters which were important, not trivial or everyday, they proved to be fruitful.

He had a very persistent feeling which was difficult to define, but very present and constant; the idea of an elephant in the room, some individual person or circumstance which was the ultimate key to the whole business and was hiding in plain sight if only he could see it.

However, the hall now loomed into view, and it was clear from the approach to it that the atmosphere had changed, or perhaps more accurately, been changed. The media representation had dwindled to no more than three or four sulky and disenchanted individuals who gave him no more than a casual glance as his car was admitted to the drive up to the hall. This suggested that none of them recognised him as the investigating officer, meaning they probably had not been here on the previous day and the media representation had been demoted from frontline journalists to the junior fringe, just told to stay there in case anything interesting happened, which they clearly didn't think likely.

The house itself was quiet, and Brigitte was clearly intending to welcome the police personnel personally this time, since she appeared in the doorway as Elaine was parking. She looked, by her standards, quite flustered, and she didn't seem inclined to waste too much time on pleasantries.

'Good morning,' she said briskly. 'Could you please come through to my office? I think we have one or two things we need to discuss.'

It was news to Max that she had an office, but the room in question, tucked away at the back of the house, was a curious mixture of business and leisure, with a large desk, a computer, a phone, files covering several shelves behind the desk, but also a comfortable-looking sofa and two armchairs in the main body of the room, which had a view of the well-tended gardens running down the side of the hall.

Brigitte ignored the desk and sat down on one of the easy chairs, gesturing to Max and Elaine to sit on the sofa. Max did;

Elaine hovered uncertainly. Brigitte, of course, knew exactly what she wanted.

'Sergeant Price, it's not for me to give out orders of any kind, but if the inspector doesn't mind, and you have no objections yourself, could you please check the state of play around our main entrance and see that whatever media people may be there are behaving themselves?'

Elaine glanced at Bellamy, and he nodded; Brigitte saw the exchange and sighed briefly. As Elaine departed, she turned to the inspector with an expression of annoyance forming on her face.

'Now please, Max, can we establish whether or not you've come here today to tell me that the investigation is closed now that the nature of my husband's death has supposedly been settled? If so, there are one or two points—'

'No, Brigitte,' Bellamy said quietly. 'That isn't what I've come here today to do, though I admit that I was afraid you might think that, or even prefer it.'

'Prefer it? Why would I prefer it? I accept that Ralph had a heart attack, as the people who are qualified to decide such things obviously think that's what happened. But I can't accept that's the end of the story. I've had a hell of a set-to with Miles and Rachel – well, mainly Miles, with only a bit of Rachel, to be honest; he decided it was end of case and he was off home, and I said if he did leave at this juncture, he needn't bother coming back at any time, and I would inform the police concerning where he'd gone. He's still here, as it happens, still chuntering and complaining. He seems to be terrified at the prospect of you talking to Rachel; why, I don't know. As far as I'm concerned, this whole business still has a ten-foot-tall question mark hanging over it, lit up in brightest neon, and I refuse to allow the premature death of a man like Ralph to simply go by default, in acceptance of his supposedly chronic heart condition. Yes, he had previously had what was described as a mild heart attack, though one of the doctors told me privately he thought it was more likely to have been an onset of angina; he was diagnosed with that some years ago and he's been on heart medication ever since, which he has taken with a minimum of fuss according to the dosage instructions. There's no evidence that anything has deteriorated since; he hasn't acquired weight, he hasn't become a gluttonous eater, he hasn't taken up smoking—'

Bellamy jumped in forcibly at this point, concluding that Brigitte's current mental state could result in her continuing in this vein for some time.

'Perhaps I didn't make myself clear, Brigitte. I'm not here to abandon the investigation; I accept that the question marks are still there, and I intend to get a few of them answered. Miles is afraid his behaviour towards his wife will come under scrutiny because of potentially violent incidents, though it's a sideshow as far as I'm concerned. He is a man with a capacity for violence, but I don't believe he had any serious wish to harm Ralph; he seems to me to be somewhat in awe of him.'

Brigitte was calmer now, and as she settled in her chair beside her very official-looking desk, she even smiled, briefly.

'Miles is something of a paper tiger, Max, to be honest, as I expect you've noticed; in terms of violence in that relationship, my anxieties would be more for Miles than they would be for Rachel. Which is another point about this investigation; there is no one in this house who has any axe to grind with Ralph – in fact, the general feeling towards him here is overwhelmingly one of respect and admiration.'

'Yes, I would accept that in the cases of those people I have spoken to. But I do need to talk to everyone else, Brigitte. Not because I really believe we have a viper in our nest; it's more a case of finding a wedge somewhere into the truth, something someone saw or knows which they don't think is significant, but probably is. It remains a death in suspicious circumstances, and my time to sort it out is now limited, so let us, please, move on quickly to arranging my interviews with the rest of the household.'

'So they're even pressurising the police, it seems?' Brigitte said, her face registering a general feeling of suspicion and distrust, directed, Bellamy assumed, at the politicians always hovering in the background.

'Well, those who regularly pressurise the police tend to be the police, unless you get to the dizzy echelons of these hierarchies, in which case, yes, it is the exalted on high making sure nothing arises to lodge nasty smells in their nostrils at the breakfast table. They filter it on down to the policemen at the top, who shovel it on to the infantry below, like me. But on this occasion, Brigitte, I can assure you that I am just as keen as anyone to establish exactly what has happened here, and I will, whether it suits the exalted ones or not.'

'Thank you, Max. I've had a feeling ever since I met you that the two of us are pretty much on the same network. I've reserved the apartment you were using yesterday for your continued use. If you tell me who's up next, I will contact whoever that might be and pass the name on to Elaine.'

So, with a feeling somewhere between curiosity and resignation, Bellamy waited in his improvised HQ for the appearance of Rachel Manningham. Once again, the sitter chose to sit in the revealing light, meaning she either had nothing to hide or she didn't realise the significance of the position in the first place. In the case of Rachel Manningham, Bellamy suspected the former was truer than the latter.

Ralph Manningham's daughter-in-law was not a woman who would immediately draw attention to herself in company. She was not beautiful and probably never had been, but she had an air of self-possession which was reflected in her neat, well-prepared appearance. As the wife of a reasonably successful husband and something of a businesswoman in her own right, she looked permanently ready to repel boarders, the boarders in this case meaning anyone intending to insult her status or presentation. She regarded Bellamy largely with a cool indifference, but he could see that there was an only slightly concealed glint in the eye which promised a big gun was there in reserve if and when it should be needed. Bellamy elected to at least begin with a conciliatory tone, even if he should come to need a big gun of his own in time.

'I'm sorry to have delayed your departure from the house for a day, Mrs. Manningham. These things inevitably take time if they're to be done properly.'

A ghost of a smile appeared and immediately disappeared on his interviewee's face.

'Oh, that was really more Miles than me, to be honest. He's been extraordinarily tedious over the last few days, I think mainly because he was actually very fond of his father, but he's the kind of man who lacks the emotional intelligence to acknowledge it to himself. He's also been rather intimidated by being understood as a violent man.'

'You wouldn't describe him as a violent man yourself?'

'No, not really. He's something of a megaphone man, is Miles. Mouth and trousers, essentially. There have been a couple of occasions when he's raised a hand to me, but raising a hand is as far as it's gone, really. I could and would flatten him if and when it became absolutely necessary.'

Bellamy, with an effort, restrained himself from an immediate response, interpreting any kind of amusement as probably untoward. The contrast between Rachel's cool imperturbability and her husband's less restrained temper became suddenly territory worthy of greater attention, including looking at it in the context of other members of the family.

'Presumably it hasn't become necessary as yet,' he said, trying hard to imitate his interviewee and therefore identify with her.

'No, though there have been one or two near misses, I would have to admit,' said Rachel Manningham. 'I'm afraid my own rather less glamorous family took a calculated risk in exposing me to the Manninghams. There was a good deal of pressure on me to bag a Manningham husband, as it were, once my mother realised that we lived within a couple of miles of the grand Manningham HQ. And Miles, in those days, was very eligible; his father's eldest son, albeit not by Brigitte, of course, though Brigitte did her best with him. Miles was tall – he still is, of course, but tall young men are a rather different kettle of fish to tall middle-aged men – and it was generally assumed that he was his father's heir. Only later did it become abundantly obvious that he was clearly not his father's favourite.'

'That being Chloe, I suppose?' said Bellamy quietly.

'Yes, absolutely. There was I thinking that I'd bagged the big one, the Manningham heir, and that's not quite what had happened. We await the reading of the will with suitable patience, of course, but I would bet almost my bottom dollar that Miles is neither the main nor the sole heir, even though the wonderful Chloe is no longer with us.'

'Did you like Chloe?'

'Does that matter?'

'In terms of this investigation, it's not yet crystal clear, by any means, what matters and what doesn't; the pointers and the relevant disclosures tend to emerge during the course of an investigation but they are often far from obvious at the start. Please bear with me for the moment. Did you like Chloe?'

'Well, now you ask, no, not very much. She knew she had her father wrapped around her little finger, and she knew well enough how her half-siblings felt about that, but it made little difference to her. Perish the thought that I should speak ill of the dead, which is why I would prefer that you hadn't asked me, but she was odd in various ways, to be honest, and she had a dismissive kind of arrogance towards those, like me, I think, who she didn't think mattered because they could do nothing for her.'

'How do you mean, "odd"?'

'Eccentric. Hardly surprising, given that her father was eccentric in his way, but his way always had some kind of purpose to it; hers just seemed generally a bit potty. She spent a lot of time up in Aitken's Wood, sometimes in decidedly Spartan conditions, and more frequently than her father ever knew, with boys. Not that I anticipate much serious hanky-panky went on; she was about three-quarters boy herself, in all honesty, and she always seemed more matey with them than anything else. I suppose it's possible that she could have been gay, but her relationships with girls seemed much the same thing; she had no time for girlie girls, of either sex, really.'

'But she was, reputedly, highly intelligent, wasn't she?'

'Quite possibly. I'm not one to judge. But given who her parents were, she could hardly be otherwise. Brigitte is near-genius, I would say, in some respects, and her father pretty much off the scale compared to normal folk. But they are an odd bunch altogether, Inspector; it always seemed to me that they lived their lives in a different place from most of us. Miles, I suppose it would be fair to say, is probably intellectually the clodhopper of the bunch, yet he is a brilliant administrator and industrialist by most people's standards.'

'And what about Anne, his sister?'

'Yes, well Anne probably isn't anyone's genius, she's more like her mother, Mary Willows. I didn't know Mary very well, but she was a strikingly beautiful woman and very sensitive, in her own way. I think she just couldn't stand the pace with Ralph and his great brain, and perhaps it was some sense of her inadequacy that partly caused her illness in the first place.'

'And while you are giving me this invaluable sketch of the family, Mrs. Manningham, what of Damien, Anne's husband?'

'Nice boy in some ways; another Chloe-worshipper in others. He was among her coterie of friends, until he started getting involved with Anne; I think he found Anne less hard work. I don't want to sound dismissive, but he's essentially a good-time boy, when all's said and done. But he was extraordinarily cut up with what happened to Chloe, so much so that I think Anne found it a bit embarrassing – and humiliating, even, to be honest.'

'What do you think happened to Ralph, Mrs. Manningham?'

Bellamy thought the abrupt change of subject might elicit a knee-jerk response which could be interesting, but he saw Rachel was perfectly capable of pausing, thinking and pointing herself in another direction when she was good and ready.

'I think he simply put too great a burden on his heart, ultimately. With a mind like his, you need to have something like a constitution to match, and he didn't have that. It wouldn't surprise me if he hadn't had a sudden, staggeringly brilliant idea which he could get his head around, but without the necessary response from his body. We shall never know now, of course. But it's not too mawkish a thing to say that his heart was well on the way to being broken as a result of what happened to Chloe.'

Bellamy found he had warmed to the woman as their conversation continued; acidic round the edges she may be, but she undoubtedly had some observations on the people around her which were worth his consideration. Chloe had loomed up in big letters before him yet again, and this time he felt he needed more information on how her life had ended.

'And what exactly did happen to Chloe, Mrs. Manningham, as far as you know? I know the basics of it; she seems to have suddenly disappeared, without anyone knowing with any certainty at all where or how it happened, and nothing has been heard of her since, in spite of professional investigators being called in.'

'That's about it. Nobody knows, even now, exactly what happened. There was a suggestion that she flew to France, but no one could prove it for definite, because no proof of her making the journey, or where she went when she got there, has ever been found. If she met with a fatal accident, either in the air or in a car, it would surely have emerged by now, likewise, if she'd been attacked by someone. It's difficult to believe that there wouldn't have been witnesses or clues somewhere along the line if that had happened, especially bearing in mind the calibre of some of the investigators. It was known that she had had a furious row with her head of research not long before she disappeared, and of course, it was becoming well known that she had some fundamental differences of opinion with her father about what the company should be doing, but none of that really seems to explain such a total and mystifying disappearance.'

Her last words hung in the air as Bellamy gave them due consideration, as he thought they deserved. Delayed physical reaction to a bereavement was far from unknown, and while Manningham would undoubtedly have used his considerable mental and intellectual resources to try and avert too drastic a reaction, it was becoming increasingly clear that Chloe was more than just a daughter. She was not only the solitary child resulting from his relationship with Brigitte Lacoste, but she was, in a way, his remaining great hope for the future. While Ralph Manningham didn't necessarily come across to him as the kind of parent who would live vicariously through his children, his own career was clearly coming to a close, mostly because of his health problems, and Chloe was perhaps all that remained of once mountainous hopes and ambitions – Chloe, who failed to agree with him on some issues basic to the future of the family business.

Chloe, Chloe, Chloe. It was beginning to seem to him that whatever direction he chose and whoever he decided to talk to, all roads continued to lead towards Chloe. For many investigations, both in his journalistic and police careers, he had been able to rely on a big flashing noticeboard suddenly appearing along the way with someone or something lit up in bright colours, and now the letters of Chloe, lit up and ten feet tall, were repeating towards him, and yet he still couldn't work out exactly what they were trying to say.

He forced himself away from his thoughts. Rachel Manningham was watching him with a slightly sardonic expression on her face; whatever she suspected, it probably wasn't anything very flattering, but nevertheless, her straight talking had been useful, more so than anyone else so far apart from Brigitte, and even Brigitte was much too involved to be able to see anything dispassionately.

'Thank you very much, Mrs. Manningham, and I think I have taken up enough of your valuable time. I am satisfied that you and your husband may leave the premises when you choose.'

As soon as Rachel Manningham had left, Elaine appeared in the doorway, with an expression which, by her standards, registered an element of anxiety.

'Detective Superintendent Hollins phoned the house about fifteen minutes ago, sir. I told him you were interviewing; he said to contact him as soon as you finished. He seemed a little – er – tense, I suppose I'd have to say.'

'OK, Elaine. I'll call you when I've finished with him. Then I would like to see Anne Atcliffe.'

Anxiety changed to doubt on Elaine's face, and Bellamy found himself wondering whether this investigation was placing an unusual strain on Elaine's usual cool competence.

'Mrs. Atcliffe has decided that she will only see you in the company of her husband, sir. I suspect it's Miles who's responsible. I didn't hear exactly what version of your meeting with him he relayed to Anne, but it sounds to me very much as if he's put it across that you gave him some kind of Gestapo going-over, and he's managed to terrify Mrs. Atcliffe with it. I've done my best to mend the damage, but Mr. Manningham can call up a storm when he's got a mind to. He would probably benefit mostly from a swift kick in the backside'

'Yes, quite possibly, Elaine. In the meantime, though, we bash on. OK, I'll see them both together. I'll call you when I've done with Hollins.'

The detective superintendent had no time for social niceties.

'Hang on to your hat, Max,' he said. 'Gregson's coming over.'

'When?'

'Now. I told him about the three days we've agreed, and he didn't dare countermand that; DCS Gregson does not care for confrontation. However, it sounds like some politico, probably this Coulson character, has been jerking his chain again, and he's made the truly revolutionary decision, for him, to get off his office arse and actually go into the field where people are doing the work, in this case Houghton Hall. I think his idea is that if he finds you twiddling your thumbs, he'll cut the three days to one or something and trump up some kind of justification for me. The powers-that-be are getting jittery about what their party donor's been up to.'

'OK, Tom. I mean, sir. Thanks for letting me know.'

'Are you getting anywhere?'

'Well, yes and no.'

'Too bloody cryptic for me, Max. I sometimes think you're being enigmatic on purpose.'

'Being more specific, sir, yes, I see some big letters lighting up in front of me, but they're not as yet accompanied by a big arrow pointing in the appropriate direction.'

'OK, I'm sure **you** know what you're talking about. Keep me posted.'

With instructions to Elaine and her assistants that even DCS Gregson should not be allowed to interrupt him when interviewing, Bellamy gently ushered Anne and her husband, Damien, into the interviewing room, and they sat on the sofa, holding hands against the big, bad man. Damien was tall and good-looking in a kind of ex-catalogue model faded into middle age way, while Anne was long-haired, big-eyed and pale, looking rather like an overgrown teenager, despite the contradictory signs of age. Damien was grinning rather forcibly, as if daring the encounter to be anything except a jolly chat between friends, and Anne was trowelling on the nervous girl too heavily and obviously for it to be credible in a woman of her age.

'We had nothing to do with any of this, Inspector,' Damien said hoarsely. 'We were just paying a routine family visit to Anne's father and stepmother.'

'In so far as you were here at the time of Mr. Manningham's death, Mr. Atcliffe, you are a witness to what was happening at the time, but no one is being accused of anything at the moment, sir; I am simply trying to establish what happened. Could you tell me whether you saw anything of Mr. Manningham after everyone had gone to bed?'

Damien looked on the point of denial, but his wife spoke first. There was an oddly babyish quality to her voice, but she spoke with some certainty.

'I saw him standing on the patio outside his study quite late on, Inspector. He just seemed to be staring into the distance. I caught a glimpse of him from our bedroom window, but I stopped watching almost immediately; it just seemed rather intrusive. And my father was never the kind of man who did things for no reason.'

'Did you watch him for long, Mrs. Atcliffe?'

'Oh, call me Anne, please, Inspector.' Her colour rose. 'No, not for long. As I said, it didn't seem right, somehow. And Damien was being – well, demanding, I suppose is the word.'

Having just about managed to get through the sentence, Anne then turned a bright shade of beetroot red, while her husband beside her was doing his best to disguise his sniggering.

Max counted twenty to himself and took a couple of deep breaths. If it was ever possible, he thought, to eliminate the irrelevant and the deliberately distracting from all the reactions people have to a crime scene, everything would be speeded up considerably. But the further into an investigation he progressed, the more inevitable it became that someone was going to have to be forced out of their comfort zone, and when that happened, revelations, or at least a valid direction, could follow. Once again, he saw the growingly demanding sign saying "Chloe", and decided to seek another reaction.

'I wondered if you could tell me, Anne,' he said gently, 'what impact you think the loss of Chloe had on your father?'

Anne's long, well-groomed hair suddenly became more visible as her head dropped, and Bellamy found himself on the end of a reproachful look from her husband.

'Bloody hell, Inspector,' Damien said. 'She's only just lost her father, and now you have to hit her with that as well.'

'I'm sorry; such investigations as this inevitably involve some difficult questions, Damien.'

'But what has Chloe got to do with it…' Damien started, but Anne's face raised, and Max saw that she had changed colour again. A boy he'd known at school, unkindly termed by some people "the chameleon", popped up in his memory. Anne had turned a vaguely greenish colour, making Bellamy wonder what habits of hers were a constant in her life style. But she seemed suddenly determined to dominate the conversation.

Which had a fair chance of working with Damien, but not with Inspector Bellamy. Anne managed two sentences of vague references to her father, both of them with the clear implication that whatever was happening, if indeed anything was happening, was a family matter and not for "intrusive eyes or ears".

Bellamy chose his moment carefully. Even as Anne was speaking, Damien seemed to be losing interest in what she was saying.

'Much as families like to keep these things "in house" in an investigation like this,' he said, cutting across Anne's attempt to restrict the investigations to "in house", 'it has to be a matter of ranging over as many issues and people as necessary to arrive at the truth.'

Damien turned to comfort his wife, and Bellamy began to get the distinct impression that there was something here into which the family didn't want him to look.

'Were you and Chloe friends, Anne?' he said, and this time the response was more vocal than physical.

'Yes, absolutely.' Anne suddenly disentangled herself fully from her husband and sat up, and now her eyes were alight, and her colour had deepened again.

'Chloe was my half-sister, but I loved her as if she was my real sister, and more so than either Miles or Rachel did. I grew up with Chloe; she was an inspiration to everyone who met her, and even though I knew my father cared for her more than he did for me, I still loved her. We used to spend hours – days, sometimes – in Aitken's Wood, and she knew the place like the back of her hand, down to those strange caves in the hill which rises on the east side of the wood. She knew the names of all the plants and trees, she knew how to build a shelter which merged into the surrounding wood so well that no one would notice it was there, and sometimes, we used to camp overnight in the place, which she could always get our father's permission to do, even if Brigitte sometimes didn't like it. And Dad, dear Dad, absolutely loved her, not in a sloppy, silly way, you understand, but in the way of liking having her around, talking to her. Whenever we were all together talking to him, we knew it was Chloe he was really talking to, and Miles resented it like hell, with being the oldest and being a boy and all that, but I didn't, because Chloe was much the best of us, and I could see that, even if Miles couldn't.'

Bellamy felt as if he had just been given a flurry of punches and been forced back onto the ropes. Here he was again, following the Chloe signs, and this one was bigger and brighter than any of the others. This wasn't just a matter of a pretty girl being the apple of her daddy's eye, this was a pointer to a remarkable, charismatic young person who impacted seriously on everyone around her, and who had suddenly and mysteriously disappeared for no obvious reason or purpose. Anne's normally placid face was alight now, and Damien was exhibiting a kind of sulky resentment, as if he was not getting the attention he deserved.

'And you, Damien? Did you know Chloe?'

'Chloe. Always Chloe. Whose death are we actually investigating here, Mr. Bellamy? Yes, I knew Chloe. Everyone here for miles around knew Chloe. I fancied her like hell, but she didn't fancy me. I don't think she liked boys – not like that, anyway, not for the sex stuff, but she knew how to get her way with them when she wanted them to do something. It was through Chloe that I met Anne, and even though Anne might put herself down, it was Anne who grabbed my attention more than Chloe did, once I got to know both of them.'

The rather forced tone of the last sentence and the occasional sidelong looks towards Anne which he made during it convinced Bellamy that Damien wasn't telling the whole truth by any means. Damien was still a good-looking man, with an easy smile and dark blue eyes in a well-tanned skin, but whether his own self-esteem was high enough for him to keep trying with Chloe when the easier and more appreciative Anne came along, Bellamy doubted. Anne, flattered by the attention, had probably been more willing to provide Damien with what he was looking for in the sexual line than Chloe, and Damien, who didn't strike Bellamy as either a deep or a devious character, was prepared to settle for what he could get.

'Thank you, both. And let me just explain, if I may, why I think Chloe is so important to this investigation; I would certainly not have asked you to revisit such a painful subject if that hadn't been the case. To understand why Mr. Manningham died in the way he did, I have to look at the priorities in his life. Even if it turns out that foul play was not involved at any stage, I need to know something about Mr. Manningham's state of mind when he died, to look at the vital clues which explain why it happened when it happened, and from all that you tell me, a daughter like Chloe must have been an enormous loss for him.'

'Oh, Chloe was much more than just a daughter to him, Inspector,' Anne said, 'and I don't mean that in any horrid or suggestive way. To him, she was his hope for the future, the one of his children with the ability to carry on what he'd been trying to do. Brigitte was his present, and he loved her for it, but Chloe was his future.'

After a few moments of heavy silence, the buzz of Bellamy's phone sounded like a rude cacophony of interruption. Bellamy closed his eyes and cursed inwardly.

'Sorry, sir,' said Elaine. 'DCS Gregson is here, and he says his time is limited. He's asking for you to meet him outside the main entrance. I did tell him you were interviewing, sir.'

Bellamy sighed long and hard. It took an effort for him not to let even the mildest curse escape him. Even so, when he glanced up, both the Atcliffes were gazing at him with some apprehension. He smiled bleakly.

'My boss has arrived, it seems, and like everyone else, policemen can't keep their bosses waiting. I'm grateful to you for talking to me, and I would be grateful if you'd stay with us for another night while I establish who I may need to talk to again. Please don't think that this is because I disbelieve you in any way or suspect you of being guilty of anything. You have helped me considerably in understanding what has been happening here and your help could be valuable again.'

The couple left with good grace, though it was obvious enough that Damien would have something to say to his wife when they were alone.

Even at this point, Bellamy was not inclined to dash towards his superior officer. He knew the kind of thing which many of his fellow officers would have to say as and when they knew that he had a decent private fortune of his own, and he had no illusions about the levels of their envy at his solid independence, but he had always contrived to remain employed and paid for reasons of self-respect as much as anything else, and something he had forgotten returned powerfully to him, something which he had dismissed at the time as irrelevant to his current and probably his future fortunes. An old colleague, old only in the sense that she and Bellamy had known each other for a long time, had phoned him out of the blue. Josie Fairbairn had been known to Bellamy for most of his journalistic career; she was the crime reporter for one of the big Midland regional papers, and she tended to be around at many of the crime scenes and interviews that Bellamy was covering himself.

He found himself talking to her one day when he'd been in his study thinking about a number of things, none of them being a return to journalism. Josie had done well for herself, as she was always going to do, and was now the editor of an even bigger Midlands daily. Josie had always been scornful of Bellamy's plans to join the police and disputed his reasoning about chasing down criminals more effectively.

'Sure, Max, you might chase a few down eventually, when you've waded through all the bureaucratic crap and the "yes-siring" to various over-pensioned idiots getting in the way, but you'd find it like running a race with your legs tied together, like you're doing the egg and spoon thing in the school sports day.'

'Over-pensioned idiots are not peculiar to the police force, Josie,' Bellamy remembered saying. 'And journos have no established legal right to arrest or question anyone. It makes a difference.'

Broadly speaking, he still considered he had been right, but now he also recalled that Josie Fairbairn had made him a generous offer, to take him on to her paper as chief reporter. As far as he knew, the offer was still on the table, and if relationships with the police big shots did start to get problematic, crossing the occupational floor once more was not out of the question. Bellamy wanted to be effective, and to do that, he knew he needed flexibility, and possibly more than the current police regime might be prepared to give him.

With a comforting feeling that he wasn't going to Gregson with his tail between his legs, and he might just have a bazooka in his armoury if he needed it, Bellamy made his way to the front entrance portico, to see Gregson standing slightly apart from an ostentatiously large car while two large, suited gentlemen stood casually watching out for their boss, though it was difficult to see what they imagined could happen to him in this place, with the media now carefully kept outside the estate walls.

Gregson's greeting was no more than a brief smile, immediately followed by what Bellamy calculated was probably meant to be a piercing glance, though having dealt with editors who made Gregson look like the local vicar, he failed to react.

'Shall we walk and talk, Inspector?' Gregson said. 'I'm always conscious that walls have ears, and especially these old country houses.'

As his superior officer started striding away, Bellamy was treated to a look at the back of Gregson's head, showing the growing stages of pattern baldness and a very obvious tension in the neck, and realised that giving way to his anger could precipitate a serious confrontation here which would serve no real purpose. He resolved to avoid it if he could, but he wasn't about to forget the bazooka, should it be needed.

'I know it's not generally the done thing, walking in on an investigation like this, Inspector, but then you don't have to deal with some of the people I have to deal with. People in very high places are breathing down my neck and appear to be getting the jitters about this whole business. When I tell you that these are the sort of people who can have a decisive say in the future careers of police officers at every level, you will realise how serious things could potentially be. As I understand it, we now know that Ralph Manningham died of natural causes, do we not?'

'Yes, sir, we do.' Bellamy bided his time.

'Which tends to be the particular aspect of this case causing the jitters in high places. Yes, it seems that Manningham had some heart issues and was taking medication, but when a still relatively young man in his mid-sixties dies in such a way, it leaves a kind of void, and our beloved media are very good at filling voids with speculation of the sort which will sell their papers.'

'Having worked on the business of selling papers myself, Mr. Gregson, I know that something like that is going to happen, regardless of what I might do.'

Gregson looked momentarily exasperated, and for a moment, his eyes met Bellamy's directly for the first time. Bellamy could already see the incipient anger in them.

'That is undoubtedly true, Inspector Bellamy, but that is exactly why we should always seek to avoid giving them ammunition. And if an issue finds itself suspended in a void, as I have already mentioned, that is more than enough invitation for them. The people in high places I referred to are very sensitive to the impressions being given to the general public, or as they see them, the electorate. Circumstances where the ruling regime of the day seems to have stopped being able to influence events create potentially the very worst void of all.'

Bellamy still held his fire, knowing that for as long as Gregson chose to talk in this way, he could always credibly claim not to have understood what was expected of him. Gregson seemed to sense this, and he began to be more specific.

'We understood that this case was finished, that Mr. Manningham had tragically died from a heart attack, a sad event in a man of such an age, but these things happen, as we all know. However, you and your sergeant and some members of the local force are still here, implying that the case is not finished and there may be nuances which make the whole business more complicated than it seems. Speculation is therefore encouraged; was Mr. Manningham in some kind of trouble? Was the trouble financial or personal? Was he severely in debt, and if so, to whom? Was he in love with someone else's partner, or someone who, for one reason or another, he shouldn't be in love with? And the fact that this man is a known donor to the Conservative Party means whatever his situation might be, the mud people will start to sling isn't just going to stick to the Manningham name, it is going to possibly cover an entire political party, with repercussions for that party's national and international standing. Do you know that a CIA agent, we understand, has now been detailed, as they call it, to keep an eye on developments in this case? Meaning it's quite possible that MI5 might be nosing around as well. If a load of grief descends on the politicians, Bellamy, you can be sure an even bigger load of grief will shortly be coming our way. Wrap it up, Bellamy, put it to bed, preferably today, and let us get on with our work.'

They had stopped walking by now, and Gregson was staring at the other man intensely, as if daring him to disagree. However, Bellamy's blood was now up, and as soon as he opened his mouth, Gregson realised this was going to be much more difficult than he envisaged.

'If that is being given to me as an order, I will tell you in so many words that my letter of resignation will be with you tomorrow, and I will then not only be talking to the press, but working with them, as a generous offer was made to me not long ago to return to my past profession in a senior and well-paid situation. And I suspect there will be a good deal of media interest in why a proper investigation of the death of a prominent and well-respected scientist and industrialist was harassed and hustled to a conclusion because of the possibility that it might upset a few Conservative politicians. Don't try to brow beat me, Gregson, I am not one of your Tory lackeys, and I know more than enough about where the bodies are buried to embarrass your tetchy masters over and beyond anything happening at the moment. Get yourself a spine, Gregson, and talk back to them. Maybe they won't be so keen on what you have to say to the papers when you've retired.'

Bellamy strode away, taking a few deep breaths as he did. He didn't look back. In the minutes it took him to return to the main entrance, Bellamy underwent one of his periodic fiercely critical self-examinations. That temper, that irrational being always lurking in the wings to suddenly elbow itself to centre stage and do whatever crazy stunt it had set its perverse mind on, had struck again. He had deluded himself that the creature had been permanently confined somewhere within him, confined so well that it would never seriously emerge to rampage around his life again. But here it was; perhaps just because of the insulation of his private fortune, he was jeopardising his police career, relying on a vague and unsubstantiated job offer to keep him employed and risking a whole lot of trouble within his relationship with a generally long-suffering partner.

And yet, and yet, a remorseless logic spoke rebellion to him. Gregson was a fool, a cypher to whichever politician, major or minor, decided to push him around a bit; he was one of those policemen who ingratiated their way to high office by yes-siring and greasing their way up the slippery pole, to find when they got where they were going that they couldn't make decisions off their own bat because they had no experience of doing so. And, of course, no one else had heard the words which had passed between them, meaning anything attributed to either of them could be denied if it had to be.

Elaine's eyes were, for once, as wide as saucers.

'What did you say to him, sir?' she half-whispered as he walked up. 'He looks like he's going to go off pop at any minute.'

'Nothing attributable, Elaine. A little local difficulty. And I think I'm now just about ready for the uncle.'

Bellamy pre-empted whatever Gregson might be thinking of doing next by marching back to the apartment where he was conducting his investigations and taking Philip Manningham with him. Of course, Manningham had a comment to make before their interview began.

'Just about time, too. I'm a busy man, Inspector Bellamy, I can't hang around this place indefinitely, especially as I'm at a loss to know why this inquiry, or whatever it is, is still going on at all.'

In the apartment, Bellamy rounded on him even before they both sat down. Perhaps, he told himself, he just needed the therapy of it, but Manningham was undoubtedly an irritating man who would probably benefit from being properly cautioned in any case, so for once Bellamy saw a way of killing two birds with one stone which worked in both the personal and the professional areas.

'This investigation is continuing because I am the officer in charge of it, Mr. Manningham, and therefore the person authorised to decide when it begins or ends. If you have a problem with that, perhaps you would like to continue our conversation in the more formal setting of a police station.'

Manningham held up his hands defensively, and he noticeably did not sit in the exposed sofa position; he chose a chair at the end of the room which was hardly lit at all. For once, Bellamy decided to take the sofa seat which allowed the light to illuminate his features – on this occasion, he was prepared to let his interviewee see his anger and impatience. The nature of this interview was not going to be dictated by Manningham, however much the man might want it to be.

'These little talks I've been having with people, Mr. Manningham, tend to be very useful in clarifying thoughts and motivations. It probably won't come as any great surprise to you that there are aspects of your relationship with your brother which concern me, bearing in mind you were telling me of his supposed treachery within minutes of me first meeting you.'

Manningham was maintaining a studied effort to remain unconcerned.

'Possibly, Inspector, though if my memory serves me right, I qualified them almost immediately with some more positive comments. And in any case, is it not now rather redundant for you to be looking for suspects and motivations when it's been established beyond reasonable doubt that my brother died of coronary heart disease?'

'Even natural deaths can have causes, Mr. Manningham. A lack of support and sympathy from those who might reasonably be expected to provide it can be one of them.'

'Ha!' From the dimness of his seat at the end of the room, Philip Manningham made a noise somewhere between a laugh and a contemptuous sneer.

'I can assure you, Inspector, Ralph was never in need of the support and sympathy of a mere mortal like me. From childhood onwards, he gave no sign of needing anything in particular from me; nor, for that matter, from his father. He was a man of positives and certainties. As I've already acknowledged, he was also a person of considerable gifts, both personally and intellectually, but neither his father nor I touched him closely at any point.'

'Will you miss him, Mr. Manningham?'

Manningham was momentarily taken aback at the question.

'To a certain extent,' he said eventually. 'And probably more than he would miss me.'

'Did you get on with your niece Chloe, Mr. Manningham?'

Again, the interviewee took a little time to respond.

'Not especially, no. I thought she was too clever for her own good. But what's that got to do with anything?'

Bellamy knew when anger was rising inside him and had also reached the age when he knew what price he could potentially pay for it getting the better of him. In younger days, his confrontation with Gregson could well have been terminal, as far as his present employment was concerned. As it was, it would probably have done no favours for his promotion prospects. His instinctive dislike for this man, so much a pygmy compared to his accomplished brother, could well have boiled over at this point, but his temper had been indulged enough for one day and he contented himself with fixing a maximum eye stare on to the man, who began wilting in the glare within seconds.

'It does rather surprise me, Mr. Manningham, that someone as close to your brother as you were fails to understand the significance of Chloe in his life. I knew Ralph Manningham vaguely before this investigation began, but it hasn't taken me very long to discover how much hope and ambition he had invested, if that's the right term, in his youngest daughter. Motivation is often an enormous part of what people want to achieve and how they set about achieving it, and most investigators would acknowledge that establishing motivation for the people involved in whatever incident they are examining is basic to the chances of success. And it is impossible to know what motivates someone without knowing their priorities and values. In the case of Ralph Manningham, they were heavily influenced by his feelings towards his daughter, and it is not in any sense a red herring to look to that for clues regarding his premature death.'

Philip Manningham had coloured slightly, but his nature seemed to be to respond aggressively, and so he did.

'I'm entirely aware of how Ralph felt about Chloe; I've known Chloe all her life. She is a remarkable person both physically and mentally, and of course any father would be proud of her. But you do need to remember, Inspector, that Ralph was a managing director and an industrialist; for most of his working life, Chloe hardly influenced it very much at all. She might be an influence, but she isn't necessarily any kind of conclusive influence. And as I happened to be looking out of a window upstairs when you and your boss, if that's what he is, were having your frank exchange of views, I'm not sure that it's your methods and priorities which will be continuing to rule the roost in this particular investigation.'

Bellamy felt suddenly very weary with the whole business. Talking to this man was not, ultimately, likely to contribute much to the investigation; like so many sibling relationships, it came with so much baggage, such a deep well of jealousies, suspicions and prejudices, that not very much of any great significance was likely to emerge. He was also impatient with himself, and in need of a period of reflection, preferably on his own. He wrapped matters up with Philip Manningham as quickly and as decently as he could, and once alone again, he found that a decision had already been made in his mind.

It meant a risk, as everything in Bellamy's life now seemed to involve a risk, but it was a course of action which might save his career, even if it could just as easily destroy it.

He would write to Gregson, at the same time as taking a few days of the mountain of leave now owing to him. Because life had been so constantly demanding for both him and Louise for so long, Bellamy had accumulated leave and, in theory at least, he could take it whenever he chose. He chose now. In his letter to Gregson, he would not on any account apologise for his remarks, but he would refer to being under considerable strain from both his superior officers and the media. He would also make a specific reference to "offers" he'd received from the media, and that would really set Gregson's pulse racing, the idea that one of his officers would suddenly decamp to the media and tell all in terms of the pressure put upon him by senior officers and the Conservative Party.

The more he considered his plan, the more he liked it. He knew there were elements in it which some would see as blackmail, but he knew equally how rough the games could get and how prepared he was to cut up rough himself if he had to. He had been put in an impossible position by being placed in charge of an investigation when many senior people, including politicians, considered there should be only one outcome, meaning the one which suited their purposes. Find out any truth as long as it's this truth, and if it isn't actually the truth, well so be it; what's politically convenient is always more important than what is actually true.

But he had people who needed to be consulted, not told, and if they didn't agree, he had to take account of their views, because he was not some pig-headed Don Quixote who carried on his crusade regardless of his allies. First, he needed to talk to Elaine, and secondly, and every bit as essentially, to Louise. Eventually, he would also need to talk to Tom Hollins, but by then his plan would have been refined and honed into a suitably streamlined form.

He realised he had been sitting in his investigation HQ, the apartment thoughtfully supplied by Brigitte Lacoste, for the best part of twenty minutes without apparently saying or doing anything. However, Elaine, at least, would not be surprised at that; she knew well enough that there had to be thinking time.

He spoke to Elaine by phone, asking her to come to the apartment, and when she arrived, he laid his plan on the line for her, initially involving three days' leave, during which he would write to Gregson and spend some time looking around the environs of Houghton Hall. Elaine sat and listened, which she was good at, and summed up her views frankly, which she was also good at.

'It's sound tactics, sir, if what you're looking to do is put yourself in a good political position. It's what you do when you get there which I would be anxious about. The advantage you will have gained over Gregson is good news for you, but not for him, and if, as is rumoured everywhere, Attorney General Coulson is breathing down Gregson's neck, he might just decide to give the whole gig to someone else, maybe even someone from the Met; it isn't exactly unknown for some supersonic policeman from the Met to be parachuted in over the heads of the country bumpkins. And then we've lost out on both counts; we're replaced on the case, and we have someone rather more high-powered than Gregson to deal with.'

'Yes, I see what you mean. So, what do we do?'

'Ask to see Gregson during your leave, perhaps, sir? I don't mean fawn to him, but just tell him why you need more time and what the potential outcome could be with a bit more time; case solved, case closed, Gregson the Attorney General's blue-eyed boy, everyone sitting pretty like kids in an ice-cream parlour.'

'Yes, and a very pretty metaphor too, Elaine. I'll ask for a meeting when I write to him. Will you take a bit of leave yourself? I don't doubt you've got plenty coming to you.'

'I will, sir. I could do with a breather.'

And you could do with a promotion, too, thought Bellamy; *the time is approaching when you still being a sergeant will be all too visibly inappropriate.* But that was not in his gift, and he didn't believe in making promises he couldn't keep.

Next up was Louise, and he remembered that tonight had already been fixed up as one of their occasional visits to a favourite local restaurant. Louise had been at a conference for the last two days and did not care for starting on meals when she arrived home from one of these events. And Bellamy was a weekend cook when he cooked at all. The probable venue they had in mind offered a decent standard of privacy and would be suitable for the purpose. He also had suspicions that there were things happening in Louise's career that she might well want to talk about.

Sitting in familiar surroundings with the woman he loved, and a few days' leave in prospect, Bellamy felt some of the clouds which seemed to have drifted into his mind in recent days beginning to lift. Yes, the Manningham case was as enigmatic as ever; the madman or genius nature of the man himself, the intricacies of his relationship with his allegedly equally brilliant daughter, the diverse and contradictory characters immediately surrounding them; sometimes, Bellamy could feel as if he himself was stuck in an ever more complex scientific maze, blundering blindly on, and always with the consciousness that he might be missing something glaringly obvious. In the background, the faceless but no less threatening high-placed politicians were waiting like unrevealed characters in the wings of a theatre, their power and influence carrying potent menace, even if still mercifully unrealised.

However, as the meal went on, it became all too obvious to Bellamy that his wife also had things on her mind. Much as their conversation remained deliberately inconsequential, Bellamy could see clearly enough that something was coming down the line. There was an extra touch of speed in Louise's tone, even a kind of breathlessness, and he couldn't help but notice that she was occasionally looking at him with something like nervousness, as if she was still nerving herself to say what she wanted and needed to say.

Only when the coffee arrived did she make herself clear, and the signals of an imminent announcement were transparent enough.

'I talked to Doug Vincent for a while this morning; it turned into an interesting conversation in a number of ways.'

She said the name with a certainty and emphasis which told him quite clearly that this was someone he ought to know. He alerted himself and rapidly searched his memory files.

'As in Doug Vincent, MP, Labour Party Chief Whip?'

'The very same. He wants me to put my name forward as the party's candidate for a constituency not far from us; actually, Max' – another quick, nervous glance – 'the one with Houghton Hall in it.'

'I see,' he said. 'And if I understand Vincent's current clout accurately, his backing would almost certainly mean you would be nominated?'

'Yes, I think so. It's what's known in the business as a yo-yo marginal, meaning it could be Labour or Tory by a few thousand, maybe even a few hundred. At the moment, the incumbent, a Tory called Sir Charles Edling who's retiring at the next election, has a majority of 674. "A big plum ripe for falling" says Doug.'

'So you want to stand, and you're wondering where that would leave me?'

'Exactly. I don't know whether you're aware of it, Max, but because of my links to Labour, I suppose, there are already whisperings in Conservative ranks that you're stretching out the Manningham case in an attempt to embarrass the Conservative Party.'

Max's left hand was on the table near to his coffee cup. Louise suddenly reached out and covered his hand with hers. He saw something like fear in her eyes and felt suddenly ashamed that she should need to feel like that.

He smiled at her and hoped that, for once, his eyes would avoid any ambiguity.

'Darling Louise,' he said. 'If you get to be a Labour MP, or for that matter even if you just stand as a Labour Party candidate, the Conservatives will say anything and everything they think they can get away with. They make fine calculations about the likelihood of whoever they're getting at bringing prosecutions against them; have the proposed targets got the money, or perhaps more importantly, the balls? In the case of you and me, my love, we have both, and I think they probably know that. Innuendo and whispers are the best they're likely to manage; if they go beyond that, well, I haven't been in both the media and the force without making a few contacts among m'learned friends, and I'd be only too pleased to sue the arse off them. The complexities of the

Manningham case are not particularly difficult to explain, and his widow has a pretty sizeable clout of her own. If you want to do it, Louise, and I think you should do it because you'd be bloody good at it, then you should go for it. I'm a big boy, and I can always get by with a little help from my friends.'

For a moment, tears welled up in Louise's eyes.

'Forgive me, Max,' she said. 'Just got to go to the girls' room.'

As she walked past him, she whispered something incredibly rude in his ear pertaining to what she was going to do to him later. Half a bottle of wine notwithstanding, his cock twitched in sympathy.

He mentally told it to behave itself until the appropriate moment and reviewed where everything stood now. As he'd said, he genuinely believed that any charges of political bias could be easily countered, and he happened to be a policeman who could defend himself in print if necessary, however many apoplexies it gave DCS Gregson. But it did mean that it would be better for all concerned if the whole case could be tied up reasonably quickly now.

And it was at that precise moment that the big Chloe arrow which had been in his mind for some time suddenly not only lit up, but started pointing in a definite direction. And when he looked to see which direction it was, an even bigger sign lit up.

Chloe Manningham, it said, *is still alive.*

PART TWO

EXILE

THREE YEARS EARLIER

Summerfield Business Village, Home Counties, thirty-five miles from central London.

Chloe Manningham enjoyed the countryside view from her second-floor office window partly for itself, but also because it represented one of her rare victories over her father. He would, if the choice was his alone, have Manningham Incorporated sited in central London, no doubt paying massive rates and rents for a huge glass and concrete box somewhere. Chloe wanted her employees to be able to breathe fresh air and enjoy a commute which would not leave them fuming with tension before their work for the day had even started.

She did try not to think of her relationship with her father as necessarily about confrontation, and there were a number of matters to do with the business where they were in general agreement. However, ever since her father had proposed that Chloe become chief executive while he took on the role of company chairman, which Chloe had agreed to with reservations she expressed at the time, there had been a number of significant differences of opinion. The theory was that Ralph Manningham would move more into the background because of his heart troubles, but the theory and the reality had not corresponded as much as they should, in Chloe's opinion.

Her father's idea of retirement and hers did not accord. For her father, it was an arrangement where he continued to take almost all the major policy decisions, even if he left the day-to-day business of executing them largely to her. For Chloe, if she was in charge theoretically, she should also be in charge practically, and hers should be the major say in choosing the future directions of the company.

And it wasn't, for her, about her abstract theory compared with her father's down-to-earth solidity, as he would sometimes hint. If anything, it was the other way round; she was centred firmly on planet Earth and believed in using the new technologies as far as possible to rescue at least part of the damage done to it, while he and his rich friends were already aiming to take the human species into the great galaxy beyond. But, of course, practicality, like beauty, is in the eye of the beholder. For Chloe, the ultimate practicality lay in doing what could still be done to rescue the planet the human species already occupied. For Ralph, it meant bowing to the inevitable and looking for homelands elsewhere.

Today, the board of the company was going to see a demonstration of how a craft, designed by the company's scientists, could use artificial intelligence and the working "operatives" – robots, functionaries, machines, whatever labels the spectator wanted to visit on them – within each landing craft to adapt and build feasible new settlements on the surface of Mars.

Chloe made her way to the project room, a large, dual-purpose chamber which allowed for the viewing of visual images of different kinds in one half of the room and discussion and analysis in the other. The viewing part was almost the size of a small town cinema, and a fair proportion of the Manningham employees in the headquarters building were usually invited to one of these major viewings, another aspect of her father's influence on the company about which Chloe was not personally very enthusiastic. The occasionally slightly frivolous "going to the movies" atmosphere at some of these events did not please her.

However, most of the Manningham workforce knew Chloe fairly well by now, and the atmosphere was subdued as she walked in. An enclosed square of seats in the middle of the viewing part of the room was kept reserved for senior executives of the company, and Chloe made her way quickly to the seat she sometimes ironically referred to as her "throne".

The lights dimmed almost as soon as she sat down, and on the screen, a large vehicle, hovering a few feet off the ground, appeared in the corner of the picture. The company's scientists had adapted the hovercraft principle, with the help of AI of course, to suit the surface of Mars, as all previous research had suggested it would be.

At first sight, the craft seemed enormous, but the figure of a man at the side of the screen made clear the scale of it, and on that basis, it didn't seem longer than about twenty feet or higher than the height of the man.

The scene shifted to the inside of the craft where a huge bank of screens was arranged along the side wall. As information about the surrounding atmosphere and terrain was displayed on the screens, a number of robot devices, most of them small and very mobile, looked to be assessing the range of obstacles near to the craft and the requirements needed for the establishment of a settlement. The devices were showing various kinds of lights and communicating with each other by sound and sight.

Words of commentary suddenly began on the soundtrack.

'The Venturer Team is currently some 750-strong, and they will not leave the landing craft until they have gathered all the information they need. They are creatures without organic parts of any kind; they need neither food nor rest. They have the capacity to increase their number at any time; they reproduce as a matter of simple manufacturing processes without any kind of sexual activity.'

The scene shifted to showing the workforce of tiny individuals now leaving the craft. Within minutes, they were beginning to build.

'By sustaining themselves with the energy sources they have discovered on the planet, the team will now begin the construction of a large building sufficient to house not only further thousands of themselves, but also substantial numbers of human beings, whose needs for air, food and movement the thousands of tiny pioneers will incorporate in the eventual central building on the planet's surface.'

The quickened film then showed the workforce putting together a covered building, with a timer in the corner of the screen going at full speed. In less than ten viewing minutes, the timer had covered ten days, and the building, compared to the outline of the human figure, was already the size of a substantial hotel.

'The pioneers are programmed to create a structure which is suitable for humans, including an atmosphere within the building which will allow human beings to breathe easily, and provisions for their sustenance and their medical support.'

Chloe listened to the commentary without comment, though her set face and tight mouth were enough to silence any comment from the other members of the board around her. Having shown the prospective outcome of the work of the AI-built "pioneers", the commentary then switched to the figure of one of Ralph Manningham's closest allies, Professor Milton Hall, who talked about the creation of the "pioneers" and the perceived advantages of them which hadn't already featured on the commentary – their size meant they could be transported for considerable distances without ruinously expensive cost, their lack of biological vulnerability meant transporting them was a much safer and easier business, and their ability to sustain themselves also by-passed any need for vast stocks of food and medical supplies. Their ability to reproduce themselves, whatever the conditions around them, also made the need for extensive follow-up expeditions unnecessary.

Hall was amiable, avuncular and with an air of easy modesty, praising the determination and dedication of the Manningham "Mars team".

'I should add,' he said, smiling to indicate, firstly, that he was coming to the end of his contribution and secondly, that he was about to introduce a rather harsher note, 'that the pioneers are well able to defend themselves should the need arise. The chances of them being interfered with by aliens from other civilisations are very low indeed, almost non-existent, in fact, going on our present knowledge of the solar system, but the possibility of difficult climatic events is a strong enough contingency to cause us to make allowances. The AI guiding the pioneers is adaptable enough for them to turn to tactics of shelter and protection if necessary, and if absolutely necessary, they can weaponise both their craft and themselves to prevent any interference or sabotage of their operations. Thank you for your attention, and I think we are looking at a very real chance that our Manningham enterprise can make a vital contribution to the continued success of mankind as a species.'

The lights went on, to reveal Milton Hall in the flesh, sitting comfortably in an armchair placed slightly to the right of the screen. He spoke to the microphone placed so conveniently before him that he didn't even need to lean forward.

'It's always essential, I think, in any of these sessions, to leave enough time to deal with the many questions which professionals in the field are bound to have about the pioneers and the implications of their work. We do not present this project as a fait accompli; while it's true that Manningham is not very far away from raising the necessary finance from various private sources to make this project a reality, everything is still sufficiently in the planning stage for adaptations and alterations to be made if they are seen as desirable. I throw open the floor to your questions.'

A tense silence followed. Most of the leading members of the Manningham board sitting to the left and right of Chloe were also equipped with microphones, but everyone knew well enough who was going to be the first person to speak. Chloe's voice, in the now silent room, was resonant and controlled enough, but the edge of anger in it was audible to those who knew and worked with her.

'Tell me, Professor Hall – Milton – if you will, please, whether there is any good reason why expeditions like this one, with your AI-created pioneers, could not also be undertaken in various situations on Earth. For example, could they be used to establish, or even create new sources of clean water in places on Earth which are struggling to find them, or could they be used to build safe and comfortable housing for over-pressed refugee settlements where large numbers of people have been displaced by war or disaster?'

Professor Hall's exasperation could only be seen in his hardening eyes; the rest of his face remained amiability itself.

'Thank you for that, Miss Manningham – Chloe. Perhaps you will permit me to say that this is an argument which we have already had on the main Manningham board. Yes, expeditions involving the pioneers are possible terrestrially, of course, but they would inevitably involve various complications. Wherever such projects are set up on Earth, they will have to be on the territory of countries which may or may not be sympathetic to the Manningham Corporation's philanthropic intentions. I'm sure you're aware, Chloe, that many African and Asian countries are not, and they might well interpret such schemes as a latter-day version of imperialism. This would put our whole operation in jeopardy, and even though the pioneers would be capable of defending themselves, the situations where they might do so would have the potential to create some very difficult international incidents. There is also the very real possibility, in the case of the water situation you were describing, for example, that dictatorial or authoritarian regimes may choose to reap these benefits for themselves, regardless of the Manningham input into such enterprises.'

For some seconds, his words hung in the air, and most eyes were turned again to the neat figure of Chloe Manningham, who was still frowning disconsolately on the whole gathering.

'Yes, there are some countries and communities which might react in such a way, but I think you know every bit as well as I do, Milton, that there are also many who would not, in countries where proper negotiations would be possible. This isn't about the practicalities of setting up projects on locations on this planet. It is an ideological matter, and it's about going for the big media-attractive options and putting up Manningham as some kind of saviour of mankind, charged with finding new worlds for us all to run to when we've finished ruining our own planet. It's about being more concerned with the big media stories than we are with serving our own people. I would also point out that projects based on Earth are instantly more affordable, and we would not have to engage in the demeaning hunting around for private enterprise funders, with all the various commercial conditions they are likely to attach to their help.'

Now the whole room was wrapped in a heavily pregnant silence, which became even more tense when the pugnacious little figure of Dr. Yvonne Silowski, Manningham's head of reseach, suddenly exploded out of her front-row seat and walked to the main presenting microphone at the front of the room. The double act of Chloe and Yvonne had form, and when it was about to resume yet again, everyone else was inclined to hold their breath or peer at what was coming next from between their fingers.

Dr. Silowski did not intend to mince her words.

'Look, Chloe,' she began, and the name sounded almost like a swear word, 'this stuff is basically between you and your dad. Let me put this in words of one syllable. Your father being chairman and you being chief executive doesn't work. Let me say that again with bells on: it DOESN'T WORK. Every time we come up with something which is ambitious, in terms of not actually happening on this planet, we have to go through this carry-on. I've been head of research at Manningham for four years, and this is about the fifth or sixth time we've gone through the same argument, and most people here don't want to argue with either you or your dad, so they make pacifying comments, or comments they hope will be pacifying, in the hope that the Manningham tug-of-war will not lose them their jobs.

'Well, the other day a very big organisation tried to headhunt me, and that's about the fourth or fifth attempt someone's made so far, so I don't give a shit any more, and I'm going to tell you where we stand. Your father has personally OK'd this pioneers project and has told us, even if he hasn't told you, that most of the funding for it is already in place. If you can't stand the idea and you want to kick it into the long grass, then call up the old man and have it out with him. Otherwise, do us all a favour and BUTT OUT!'

For several seconds, Chloe found herself struggling for breath. It seemed to be a case of "pass the parcel", she felt, and the parcel was her. She would make her points to her father, and he would listen politely, say his piece and then tell her to take it up with the research people. So, she would take it up with the research people, and they would tell her to take it up with him. She was conscientiously trying, as far as she saw it, to do what she had been appointed to do, point Manningham in constructive and modern directions, and her father had turned it into an obstacle race, his various appointees being the obstacles.

By the time she had controlled her anger and her breathing for long enough to begin talking into her microphone again, the meeting had started to split up, and she saw that Yvonne Silowski was saying no more than the truth; no one wanted to be around when the Manningham dynastic tussle broke out all over again.

On either side of her, Chloe's assistants and supporters were standing up and trying to stop the research team from drifting away. For one furious moment, she contemplated stamping her foot very loudly to signal to everyone concerned that the meeting was not over, and she had not finished speaking. But everyone was now almost stampeding for the exits, and she registered that she needed to take Silowski's threats seriously; she knew the efforts her father had made to bring the woman to Manningham in the first place, and how infuriated he would be if she resigned; as she would. Whatever Chloe thought about Yvonne Silowski, she knew she was no bluffer.

Back in her office, Chloe asked everyone to leave and tried to think through what she could do next. The contradictions and problems seemed to be tearing her mind apart. She could demand Silowski's resignation, though she had to acknowledge to herself that the head of research might already have decided to resign anyway; after the speech she had just made very publicly, she might decide there was little else she could now do. Chloe tried to visualise a contrite Silowksi on the phone, asking for a meeting and apologising for having got carried away in reaction to what Chloe felt were perfectly reasonable questions, but she knew Yvonne Silowski better than that.

After some minutes, Chloe became aware of an intense headache, and she had to admit to herself that, for once, she didn't know what to do. Once again, she could phone her father and once again, point out her anxieties and problems concerning their joint management of Manningham Corporation, with a view to getting him to finally realise that the division into chairman and chief executive was not working and probably never would. But that, of course, would mean that he would both have to acknowledge that he had been wrong in the first place to establish such an arrangement, and also be prepared to effectively hand over control of the organisation to her, reducing himself to an impotent figurehead by his own actions.

Chloe's headache intensified. They had backed her into a cul-de-sac, she felt; they had conspired and contrived to try and make her see her own irrelevance to the issues. And the family no longer maintained cohesive control over the events leading up to the pioneers project, chiefly because its two chief members were quite deliberately at loggerheads with each other.

Chloe became conscious that her eyes were closing and the noises around her were tailing away. Try as she might, she couldn't stop her headache deteriorating further and a sense of both physical and mental weakness overtaking both her body and her mind. Now she could hear nothing at all but the sound of her own laboured breathing, and all consciousness of where she was and what was happening around her drifted away.

She woke slowly, trying to relate the surroundings she was now seeing to what she could remember had been there in her earlier consciousness. As her eyes opened, a sudden sense of panic seized her; she seemed to be sitting in a public place, a tree-lined square which appeared to be, judging by the noises of traffic and human voices, in the middle of a city. And somehow, though she couldn't begin to understand how, she knew that the city was Paris. From her bench, she could see a street sign on one of the nearby buildings saying *Place Vendôme*.

Was she dreaming? Was she hallucinating? Like many young people of her generation, she had experimented with taking various substances in the past, but that was some time ago; such a long-delayed reaction was impossible to understand. But, unless this was some kind of dream, she had no idea of how she had come to be here. She had a vague sense that some time had passed, but no sureness or certainty about how long it had been or how she now came to be here.

Sitting outside a café not more than a hundred yards away, a man in his early thirties was enjoying a morning coffee with his edition of *Le Monde* when he caught sight of an attractive, wide-eyed young woman sitting on a bench. He glanced at her for a moment, and then turned back to his paper. Staring at women in the street was not a pastime he allowed himself. A glance, perhaps; a cat, after all, can look at a king, but no fixations, no intrusive behaviour. But then, he was a doctor and it seemed to him that the woman was in shock about something or other, and this particular young man knew quite a lot about people being in shock.

Jean-Claude Menteau came back to Paris whenever the opportunity arose, to spend his leave relaxing as well as he could in the beautiful environment of a city for which he had a particular affection. The rest of the time, he worked for an organisation called Médecins Sans Frontières, known in English as Doctors without Borders, going to whichever parts of the world required his services, usually, but not always, French-speaking countries. Jean-Claude had a passable grasp of English, but he preferred his native tongue, and especially in the kind of circumstances where he often found himself working. Currently, he was working in Mali, amongst migrant camps, where inadequate numbers of medical practitioners were trying to deal with huge numbers of people with all kinds of problems. Two years ago, Jean-Claude had been only yards away from a serious conflict between Islamist militants and the Chadian Army. He had picked up infections from his patients on more than one occasion and had, rarely and uncharacteristically, almost come to blows with supporters of Marine le Pen.

He was a dark-complexioned, slimly-built man – had he ever had the tendency to put on weight, his occupation and his working hours would have taken care of that – and he had occasionally been described as good-looking at the university where he trained and in his subsequent work, though had anyone described him as such to his face, he would have been rather taken aback. His digestion had suffered a good deal from the unfamiliar diets of his working environments, and strictly speaking, coffee was a drink which he would do better to leave alone, but coffee went so splendidly with a few days of quiet leave in Paris that he was unable to stop himself.

Dealing so frequently with frightened, displaced and anxious people had made him an expert in spotting such symptoms, and it was clear enough to him that the woman he was looking at, notwithstanding her expensive clothes and good looks, was clearly quite seriously disturbed by something.

The French equivalent of "mind your own business" sounded in his mind; he was in Paris to take it easy, have time off, get to know all over again what being in charge of his own time and leisure was about, not rush off to lend probably unwanted assistance to damsels in distress. But then, and quite suddenly, the young woman tried to stand up and almost immediately tottered, very nearly falling over one end of the bench, and Jean-Claude was much too much the gallant Frenchman to allow such things to happen without at least offering some help.

By the time he approached the woman, several other people seemed to have noticed her; she was now holding desperately onto the arm at the end of the bench in an attempt to support herself.

Jean-Claude hesitated; in Paris, someone could be almost any nationality in the world. He decided to address her in French, in the hope that she was French, and therefore easier.

'Forgive me, *mademoiselle*, but you seem unsteady; may I help?'

Chloe heard the words, and realised, inexplicably, that she could speak French, but how she had come to be able to do so, she had no idea. In spite of being unaware of who she was or where she came from, it seemed that she could speak French.

'You are very kind, *monsieur*; I am not sure where I am, or who I am, for that matter.'

Jean-Claude sat down on the bench beside her. He was only thirty-four years old, but he had already seen more than enough to know that the process of calming a situation down could be more easily achieved by removing the drama from it as soon as possible.

'Perhaps it might help if we went somewhere for a quiet cup of coffee, away from all these people busy gawping at you.'

He began to move away from the bench, and Chloe, gradually at first but then with greater confidence, followed him. They left the main square, and found a quieter street nearby, where they sat just outside the café and Jean-Claude ordered coffees and cognacs.

'May I use your name, *mademoiselle*?' he said quietly.

'Erm…' Chloe shook her head dumbly; tears began to rise to her eyes.

'*Monsieur*,' she whispered, 'I don't know it.'

'Then we will try and wait until you have a greater power of recall, hopefully soon.'

Chloe felt reassured by the man's easy manner and unruffled reaction to a situation which he cannot have been used to. But he was French, and darkly handsome, and she was somewhere without knowing how she had got there and why; panic was only just under the surface. All the cards were in his hands, and this wasn't a situation she would normally countenance for a minute.

'You seem to be a pretty unruffled character, *monsieur*. Are you used to running into people who have no idea who they are?'

'Well, in a way, I suppose I am. Mostly they know who they are, or they can just about remember when prompted, but they are often displaced and lost, with everything they used to know and rely on completely dispersed.'

He went on to describe his current work in a refugee camp in Mali, without dramatising or embroidering the facts of it, and she appeared to be interested in spite of herself. By the time she had had the coffee and the brandy, she was more composed and relaxed, but she still seemed to have no recollection of where she had come from and who she was.

Jean-Claude registered the quality and cleanliness of her clothes, and the fact that she was wearing make-up. She was quite clearly not a vagrant or a tramp; he had known many examples of such people, and this young woman did not come into that category in a whole range of ways. She spoke French with remarkable fluency, but to Jean-Claude, whose work involved listening to people of many different nationalities talk French, she had a slight but detectable English accent. The business of traumatic memory loss was by no means unknown to him; some of the refugees he had met in various camps had seen and heard things which no one should ever see and hear, and the reaction of some had been to blot such memories out or adapt them to being something else less horrendous. Total refusal to acknowledge what they had been through was rare, but not that rare.

Chloe felt a deep sense of gratitude to this kindly-disposed man, but she was aware of her very vulnerable situation; she had no recollection of having booked into a hotel or apartment, or why she was in Paris at all. To meet this knight in shining armour was a relief, but then he came out with a remark which immediately aroused her suspicions.

'This is still quite a public place, *mademoiselle*. I have an apartment booked in Paris, not far from here, for the duration of my leave; it is comfortable and private, which will enable us to have a private conversation and help you get your bearings.'

Whatever else Chloe had forgotten she could still remember the tactics of men.

'OK, *monsieur*. And how else, I wonder, will you decide to help me get my bearings?'

Jean-Claude looked discomfited. He had to offer an explanation, and that inevitably meant going over ground which was still painful.

'I should perhaps explain that I have been bereaved quite recently of my wife Madeleine. Recently meaning just over two years ago now, which doesn't sound too recent, I suppose, to some, but to me, I suspect it will still seem recent in another five years. Madeleine was also a doctor working for MSF, and a little older than myself. The kind of work we do means we have to try to be extra careful to protect ourselves from the various afflictions which stalk the camps; we do try, as far as possible, to live at a reasonable distance. My wife was very conscientious and involved, perhaps too involved—'

Jean-Claude turned his face away momentarily and struggled to control his voice.

'She might be said to have not been as scrupulous in her precautions as she should have been, but she was a very committed professional, as everyone knew. She eventually succumbed to illness when her immune system had already been considerably weakened.'

'I am so sorry to hear that. I cannot properly introduce myself, *monsieur*, but perhaps you would be kind enough to do so?'

'My name is Jean-Claude Menteau. And I really must call you something; men should not address ladies anonymously. If you can't remember your name, perhaps I should call you a suitable French name? Would you object to Jeannette? I have a cousin of that name.'

'No, Jean-Claude. I would be happy to share your cousin's name.'

'My apartment has two bedrooms. There are sometimes occasions when a member of my family is able to join me on my leave in Paris, most commonly my younger brother, Henri. But he is wrapped up in examinations, the curse of university students of his age, and hasn't been able to join me this time. I still have a week and a half of my leave, and perhaps that might be long enough to restore your memory, or seek professional help; whatever it is you decide to do.'

Jean-Claude's apartment turned out to be in the Latin Quarter, and before they eventually reached it, he had shown Chloe some of his favourite parts of the city. After a few hours, Chloe was beginning to feel that Paris was, somehow, not as unfamiliar as her total loss of memory might suggest – unsurprisingly, as she had been there with her mother, Brigitte, many times, not always with her father as well.

It was both frustrating and frightening; reliable recollections constantly seemed close enough to need no more than a few minutes of intense mental activity. But try as she might, nothing specific, definite or undeniable was revealed.

Out of the public eye at last in Jean-Claude's hired apartment, the two of them suddenly found a certain shyness in each other's company. Conversation became rather strained, as Chloe had no reliable memories she could talk about, and Jean-Claude was dealing with the unfamiliar situation of having a woman who was not Madeleine in his private quarters.

Paris and Madeleine were the only two subjects they were able, at this stage, to talk about. The latter was too painful for Jean-Claude to concentrate on for any length of time, but the former seemed promising; it had already become apparent that Chloe was not a total stranger to Paris by any means.

'Can you remember who you were with when you came to Paris?' Jean-Claude asked.

'That is the most frustrating thing. I can hear something of the voice, and even some details concerning where we went. But no more than that.'

Over the next week, the two of them grew closer together. Jean-Claude was beginning to realise how lonely his life was, even, or perhaps especially, when he worked in the company of many other people. He also grew to understand how much he missed being in the intimate company of a woman, and even as he felt pangs of guilt that the woman wasn't Madeleine, he knew that the huge gap she had left in his life had to be at least partially filled sooner or later if he was not to spend the rest of his life as a semi-hermit.

For Chloe's part, she had had a few male lovers in the past, though none of them had made themselves precious or indispensable to her. She had always liked the company of men, as she had once liked the company of boys, but only if a relationship could be conducted on equal terms, and liking their company didn't necessarily mean liking the idea of sexual intimacy with them.

But she had only been with Jean-Claude for four or five days before she started acknowledging to herself that she not only liked but also fancied him. He was meticulous in not imposing himself upon her; if he needed to have a shower or a bath, he would wear a long dressing gown to move from his bedroom to the bathroom and back again and would not emerge from his bedroom until he was fully dressed. She had to concentrate on behaving in a similar way, even though she felt instinctively that her normal regime, much as she had forgotten it, was probably more relaxed and slapdash than his.

And she felt, displaced and confused as she was, that she needed someone to make love to her, not least because of the possibility that becoming a lover again might break whatever dam had built itself in her mind and stopped her from remembering who she was.

Jean-Claude, for his part, was in agonies of indecision and not a little guilt. He had no knowledge of who this woman was, he would say quietly to himself at times; she was clearly ill in some unspecified and largely mental way, and she needed to seek and get professional help to restore her memory. It was perfectly possible, in fact probable was a more likely word, that she already had a partner, husband or lover; for such a woman to be entirely alone in the world made no sense at all. If and when her memory was restored, what would her family and friends, let alone her husband or lover, think of this person who had taken advantage of her mental state to make himself her lover?

But maybe, another and very compelling voice argued, Madeleine had, at long last, faded into a memory. Maybe this woman coming into his life had been meant to happen, because the more time he spent with her, the more he loved her. It had already become clear that she was a competent and highly educated scientist; what she had re-discovered about herself was already extensive, and it seemed an extraordinary prospect to contemplate what the entirety of her might amount to.

And the more he got to know her, the more attractive she became to him. To lose so much of herself would have been crushingly daunting for many people, but not for Jeannette; she was still vivacious, intelligent, sometimes almost unbearably sexy, and when he recalled how long it had been since he last made love to a woman, who had, of course, been Madeleine, he realised that a force was growing within him which might soon become more than he could control.

They had been together for eight days, with the prospect of his leave coming to a close within another couple of days, when the inevitable happened, and predictably enough, it was Chloe who took the initiative.

They had been travelling around Paris all day, simply drifting from place to place and watching the world go by. Jean-Claude prepared to take his early-evening shower, before they decided what they were going to do with the evening. When he returned to his bedroom and began to take off his dressing gown, he saw that Chloe was lying on the bed in her underclothes.

He licked his lips and swallowed hard. She moved towards him. Nothing, it seemed, needed to be said by either of them. She undid the dressing gown cord around his waist, and edged the gown off his shoulders, until it fell to the floor, and he stood, completely naked, in front of her. She kissed him, and her hands caressed his body, not shying away from the most intimate areas. After only a moment's hesitation, he returned her kiss, and gently removed her clothes in his turn. By the time Chloe was naked, his involvement and enthusiasm for the proceedings had become abundantly obvious, and he had decided that his period of mourning and desolation had gone on for long enough, and perhaps longer than was mentally or physically good for him.

They made love slowly, gently and carefully, as if enjoying and wishing to relish a good meal after such a long period of abstinence, and the experience worked so well for both of them that, after a suitable rest, they did it again.

Only then, while in the process of enjoying glasses of good wine, did they pause to reflect how this had changed the situation. The plan which had been at the back of Jean-Claude's mind for some days, which was to persuade Chloe to go with him to the nearest offices of the gendarmerie so that she could begin the process of tracing what had happened in her life, seemed already redundant, as it would mean that he might never see her again, and at the moment, that idea had become unbearable.

For Chloe, Jean-Claude was the only solid reality in a world which had become a vague, mystifying mass. Her mind tantalised and tortured her, both awake and asleep, with vague visions and memories of people she didn't know and places she couldn't remember. She reasoned that something in her past life must have been grim, unacceptable or totally self-defeating to have had the effect of wiping her mind clear. Returning to her past life might well mean confronting whatever had caused her breakdown, blackout or whatever it was, and perhaps there was every possibility that what had happened to her mentally once might happen again.

Perhaps the sudden blank cheque that had been presented to her was actually a golden opportunity to point her life in a completely different direction. Perhaps Jean-Claude Menteau was, quite literally, a blessing in disguise, and there was some deeper meaning to why the two of them had been accidentally thrown together in the way they had, Jean-Claude because he had been unable to restart his life after the loss of his Madeleine, and herself because the life she had been living contained something or someone which she simply could no longer live with.

But, of course, preparing a future with Jean-Claude was full of various problems, and some of them could be insurmountable. In a few days, he would leave the comfort and relaxation of his holiday in Paris and return to Mali and his work. Chloe could only guess at what such a job might entail and how she could possibly fit in to such a set-up. As far as Jean-Claude's professional colleagues were concerned, Chloe could only be some piece of human flotsam and jetsam which he had carelessly picked up as a lonely man drifting around Paris. She would stick out like a sore thumb, and perhaps find herself simply moving from trying to deal with one impossible life situation to struggling with another.

Jean-Claude, however, was a starving man who had just feasted, and had already made up his mind not to return to his starvation. It was as if he had been rattling around, going through the motions of life, while completely empty, vacated of all feeling and excitement, and suddenly everything had returned with a rush – a woman he could love, and a life which once again had a meaning. Even though he knew, by any normal process of logic, that Chloe's memory would return, and there could be a whole catalogue of people and circumstances in her life which might reclaim her and exclude him, he felt that what they had established between them would not disappear or be suddenly excluded easily. He saw himself standing on the edge of a leap of faith, with life daring him to jump, and for once, his cautious, self-effacing nature was prepared to take on the challenge.

'If I went to Mali, what could I do, Jean-Claude? Be the mysterious woman in your life who has materialised from nowhere, and is so vacuous that she doesn't know who she is or where she's come from? You and your colleagues will be doing difficult, challenging work and I would be some drifter in your life, the left-over from a holiday romance.'

'Not if you were my wife, you wouldn't.'

She glanced across at him. He was still naked, his long, beautifully proportioned body occupying the full length of the bed. He seemed to have made his extraordinary statement in all seriousness, and she already knew him well enough to know that practical jokes, and particularly this kind of practical joke, were not his style at all.

'Let me fully understand, Jean-Claude,' she said. 'You are proposing to me?'

He turned to her, and she saw the captivating smile which he rarely used appear once again.

'Yes, I am. My work is difficult, Jeannette, both physically and emotionally; I have been coming to the realisation in recent months that I am not going to be able to do it for much longer without something changing, even though I struggle to identify and decide exactly what. It is the kind of job which demands that you have someone to go home to, not just a place you call home, but a place with a person in it who can put in you the mettle and the stamina to carry on. Working for MSF is not something I will do for the rest of my life; some people do, I know, but they must be stronger and more resourceful than I am. My present contract has two more years to run, and then I think I will have to spend some time in France, working at something which is easier to cope with.

'Perhaps, by then, your memory will have returned, and perhaps the people in your life who have been forgotten for the moment will not forgive me for taking advantage, as they see it, of your reduced state. But even in the short time I have known you, it has become obvious to me that you are an extraordinary person, because even though, at the moment, only half of you is conscious and alive, you are still huge enough to fill my life and suddenly put back what I have been missing so badly. Perhaps, by the time you are whole again, so will I be, and then we can look at where and who we are and decide where to go next, but for the moment, we are doing each other such an enormous amount of good that I cannot just back away from it and pretend it never happened. Can you?'

'No, my love, of course I can't. I have nowhere else to go, I know that, but at the moment, there is nowhere else I want to go. Something happened in my life, something apparently so difficult for my mind to deal with that it seems to have wiped my memory. Sooner or later, everything will come back to me, and I will have to face again whatever I could not face before, and if I am to do that, something good needs to have happened to me to give me the strength I need.'

Marriage was agreed between them, to their mutual astonishment, but once that goal was decided upon, the practicalities had at last to be faced, and difficulties arose almost immediately, as Chloe realised that what Jean-Claude had in mind seemed to involve the two of them living separately for the first few months of their marriage.

'I cannot take you to Mali. It is a very poor and, in some ways, a very dangerous country, and in your present vulnerable state of mind, the pressure on you to make some kind of life while I am working would become unbearable. I have built up a good deal of leave in the time since I lost Madeleine, because it seemed pointless to be taking leave when there was nothing for me to do. I had to be persuaded into this trip to Paris. My earnings have built up, because I have very little to spend money on where I am; MSF provide my basic food and lodging, and a social life, except on a very minimalist level, has had no attraction for me. In any case, providing a narrative to explain who you are is not too difficult in France; people will accept you as my wife, and until your memory returns, we can put together

– what's the best term for it? A Hinterland? A back catalogue? – enough to say who you are and how you came into my life. I know you speak English very well; I've heard you do it a few times when we've been wandering around Paris and you come across British tourists. But if it came to you leaving France, all sorts of additional information would be required. I take it you don't know where your existing passport is?'

Chloe was momentarily too dejected to answer. It seemed so deeply infuriating that even a little basic paperwork to assist her in jogging her reluctant memory was not available. For some minutes, the two of them fell silent, as if the business of facing their future together had conjured up a whole mass of questions and problems to be thought about and resolved.

'So,' she said eventually, 'I will need to stay in France, and live on my own while you work out the rest of your Mali commitment. We will have to be content with seeing each other on your leave periods. It will mean living in the deep south of France, so that your journeys home can be as uncomplicated as possible.'

Jean-Claude looked relieved and smiled.

'Yes, that's exactly what it does mean, and of course, as I suspect you usually do, you have thoroughly worked the whole thing out in a matter of minutes.'

The remaining days of Jean-Claude's leave were spent deciding on somewhere in France to make a home, and the ultimate decision lay with Jean-Claude, as he had a much more thorough working knowledge of the country than Chloe did. He had spent an enjoyable three years working in Marseilles before he decided to apply to Médecins Sans Frontières, and he had been particularly enchanted with the Le Panier district of the city, a picturesque and historic area which even the endless tourists could not ruin.

After a long, painful leave-taking, Jean-Claude headed back to Mali and Chloe, backed with enough money to secure a property she felt adequate, headed south towards Marseilles.

And it was while Chloe was booked into a modest hotel in Le Panier, still amazed at everything happening to her even as she scoured the local papers and the *immobiliers,* that a tense meeting was taking place in the resplendent main lounge of Houghton Hall.

Ralph Manningham, looking pale and tired, occupied his favourite enormous armchair which looked towards the view on the south side of the hall. Brigitte, who hid her rising panic as well as she could, which was very well by most people's standards, was lounging on the sofa to his right, and in the armchair facing him sat a well-dressed large man, tanned enough to indicate a largely outdoor life, who was clearly not at his ease.

Sam Key was a private investigator, and when first appointed to this current job, he could hardly believe his good luck. He had been in the investigation business for nearly ten years, after a short police career which ultimately tired and frustrated him, and he was now in his late thirties. Most of his business consisted of tracing people, and while he steered very clear of searches where the person or persons commissioning him were aiming to do damage or gain revenge on someone, he was prepared to have a try, however obscure or challenging the searches might be. He had worked for a number of rich men and women in his time, but this was the first one who actually had a "sir" in front of his name, and much as he believed in an egalitarian approach to life, this client and his sophisticated wife were a little overawing for him. Taking the case on had not worried him at all in the first instance, as he calculated that someone as widely known as Chloe Manningham was unlikely to be able to hide herself from the world very effectively, but he hadn't allowed for the lady's extraordinary thoroughness in covering her tracks when she didn't want people to know where she was.

'As I mentioned on the phone, Sir Ralph, your daughter seems to have a record of being very determined that no one should know where she is. I've previously mentioned to you that she apparently had an extremely outspoken set-to with the company's head of research, Dr. Silowski, and I think you are familiar with the details of that particular difference of opinion.'

'I'm afraid I'm probably responsible for it,' Manningham said quietly, and Brigitte glanced across at him with some concern.

'Well, we know about the argument, or probably more accurately, the shouting match, and we know that Chloe left suddenly and impulsively not long after that. However, she habitually uses a small plane to travel, and I do mean small, because she is genuinely concerned, as you know, to keep her carbon footprint respectable. Her pilot, who is privately employed by her rather than the company, has been told, even on pain of dismissal, not to reveal her destinations. Apparently, she quite frequently travels incognito, sir, because she doesn't necessarily want other companies to know where she's going and why. It's not that uncommon for people in her situation, but she seems to take it to quite stringent levels and given the considerable public profile she's had ever since becoming chief executive of Manningham Corporation, it's probably understandable on most levels. We've managed to lean on the pilot sufficiently to get him to reveal her destination, which was France, on this occasion. They landed at an airfield somewhere in Normandy, though all our pressure so far has been unable to get him to reveal where exactly this was. He insists that he wants to retain his job, and he clearly has a deep sense of loyalty to your daughter, sir, which is fair enough, but not much use to us at the moment. Where she went after making this landing, we simply haven't been able to trace. France, of course, is one of the safest countries in the world, but when someone is in a distressed and anxious state, as I'm afraid to say she probably was – she herself appointed Dr. Silowski as head of research, I gather – it's very difficult, in fact almost impossible, to say exactly what she will do and where she will go.'

'Didn't she make any arrangements with this pilot for him to meet up with her later?' said Brigitte, as her husband stared fixedly out of the window.

'She made a vague statement to the effect that she would phone him, Lady Manningham. It would be fair to say that the pilot is in something of a state; he keeps saying she had a weird air about her, almost as if she was sleepwalking, he says. He refers to how easy she generally is to talk to, and how she is quite often in the habit of asking him about his wife and kids, but there was none of that this time. He comes across as being resentful, as he puts it, to "whoever put her in a state like that".'

'Oh God,' said Ralph, and suddenly walked towards the window, looking out at the scenery without moving.

'Thank you, Sam,' said Brigitte. 'Please keep us in touch if there are any further developments. We'd like you to stay with the case for the time being, if you will; I'll see to it that you are provided with further funds so that we can keep up the search.'

'OK, thanks,' said Sam, and took his cue to leave with some relief.

'Goodbye, Sir Ralph,' he said on the way out, but it was only when his hand was actually on the door handle to leave that Ralph Manningham responded.

'Yes, goodbye, Sam, and thank you,' he said, without looking round.

Brigitte moved towards her husband and put her hand on his shoulder. As he turned to her, she could see the trace of tears in his eyes.

'I told Silowski to be gentle in the presentation of this. That's why I suggested Milton Hall should be in charge of the presentation itself. Silowski seems to have gone out of her mind, just because Chloe asked a few questions.'

'Two bosses, darling. I know you keep saying that wasn't how it was envisaged, but that's how it's turning out. It isn't so easy in practice to divide up authority and responsibility as it looks in theory.'

Ralph turned away from the window and both of them sat down on the sofa, facing each other.

'I said to her, Brigitte, in words of one syllable, that the only thing I wanted to continue doing as chairman of the company, beyond being a figurehead when needed, was to OK a few space research projects. I gave over to her the entire administration of the corporation, or rather the more complicated stuff which wasn't in the remit of Miles, the whole hiring and firing thing, most of the supervision of the company's finances, everything. I just wanted to hang on to a few of the forward projects, the stuff which will take the company into the whole business of finding new living spaces for the human race, which is becoming more urgent year by year. I haven't said anything to stop her pursuing terrestrial projects if she thinks them justified.'

'If she knows what the money situation is, she might have decided both are not feasible, and it has to be one or the other. Meaning she has to give way to your research vision or do nothing at all in that particular line,' Brigitte said.

'Well, perhaps. But if that's what she thinks, why hasn't she told me?'

'I don't know, darling. Maybe it's all been too much too soon. She seems to have blown a fuse big time, and when that happens, it's usually when things have been boiling up inside for a good while.'

Ralph sighed. 'Well, when she reappears, we'll re-define everything. Maybe I'll split off and start a separate company, without raiding Manningham funds. I've got some promising contacts. Perhaps keeping the politicos happy might finally yield something. UK-leading international space research, breakthrough on the Moon and Mars, who needs the Americans anyway, all that kind of nationalist drivel; they'll lap it up. I could finish up in the

Lords, lucky me, doing what the Chief Whip tells me. Voting to order. Trotted out pre-election to tell the electorate what a super technological society their government is heading. God, how I hate that stuff.'

'And Chloe, as you well know, is Labour and probably always will be. You might find yourselves on election specials arguing the toss with each other.'

'Maybe. For the moment, Brigitte, I would happily settle for knowing where the hell she is.'

For a moment, words failed both of them. They held on close to each other.

'Sam knows what he's doing,' Brigitte said, in almost a whisper. 'We should have some answers soon. It often seems as if there's no answer that makes any sense, but more often than not, there is. I don't believe that Chloe would deliberately set out to hurt or worry either of us and I don't think you do either. We'll know soon, darling.'

The day before Jean-Claude departed for Mali, he and Chloe were married in a small Paris office. Jean-Claude flatly refused to inform any of his relatives about what he was doing, and his relatives appeared, in any case, to be rather thin on the ground.

'My mother died when I was seventeen; it was mostly the inadequate attempts the medical profession made to identify her cancer and treat it before it was too late which drove me into medicine in the first place. My father and I are more or less estranged; he married someone else with what I considered to be unseemly haste, though I was in several kinds of mental turmoil at the time. He subsequently refused to allow for that; he decided I was being a little prig and he and his new love cut off contact. I wasn't in the mood to make it up, and I certainly wasn't going to apologise, so it remains broken to this day.

As I told you before, I have a younger brother, Henri, who did for a while try to bring my father and I back together, young as he was and is, but after he left home to go to university, his mind was elsewhere. We meet and dine together from time to time, but I would no more consult him on who and when I intend to marry than I would the youngest nurse in my hospital.'

Jean-Claude caught sight of the dejection of his bride-to-be and made an effort to be more upbeat about the whole matter.

'When I leave MSF, Jeannette, when we have much more time to play with, then we will try and arrange a proper ceremony. In the meantime, let's do it while we can and start a new life for both of us.'

Chloe found herself looking for accommodation in Marseilles while letting a small flat for a few weeks. However, Jean-Claude hadn't left the whole business entirely to his new wife. He had contacted an old colleague of his who had lived in Marseilles all his life, and he was able to give Chloe, in her Jeannette alias, a good deal of help with likely contacts. His occasional random questions of her, Chloe could deal with, after she and Jean-Claude had settled on a few details of her past life, including a few allowances for what Jean-Claude heard as her English accent. The friend, Charles Carsaillon, now a consultant, took the situation at face value and his questions were not too intrusive or difficult.

Settled into a new life and enjoying what she still tended to think of as a release from whatever pressures had taken her memory, Chloe devoted herself to her task and soon had taken on a modest two-bedroom apartment in an area not far out of Le Panier, which Charles told her was "very touristy". Charles visited her and helped her to set up the apartment. Chloe grew to appreciate him largely because he was not only very competent in dealing with people and in his knowledge of the city, but also not about to judge her or interrogate her.

Two months after returning to Mali, Jean-Claude came back on his first leave. He had only ten days available and had spent most of the first two travelling. However, exhausted as he was, he expressed delight in what had been achieved in the choice of apartment and Chloe's efforts to make it as comfortable as possible. They spent a blissful three days relaxing and making love, and then spent a whole day exploring the area where they now lived, including the multitude of cafés and restaurants of all shapes and sizes.

Then, to their mutual distress, Jean-Claude had to return to Mali, though before he went, he was able to mention that the two remaining years on his contract might be shortened by up to six months.

'They are very aware of burn-out issues,' he said. 'I know you said you would be willing to go to Mali with me for a while, my darling Jeannette, and I am truly grateful to you for being prepared to undertake such a thing, but the accommodation you would need to live in would be very basic, and I think there is likely to be quite a lot about the country's attitudes to women you would find difficult to live with. You have been through enough, my love. Sooner or later your memory will start to return, and when that begins to happen, we will have already built for ourselves a firm enough foundation to withstand whatever we face.'

After Jean-Claude returned to Mali, some vague memories did start to form in Chloe's mind, even though she found herself trying to mount a resistance against them; her present life seemed to offer much more than her past life had done, and she felt increasingly reluctant to encourage a process which might ultimately destroy what she had set up with Jean-Claude. She had occasional visions when she did her spasmodic wandering about in Le Panier, of being in France before with an older woman who was actually French herself and who was related to her in some very direct way. There was also a vague and slightly menacing male figure lurking in the background, though no more concrete than a shadow in the wings of the stage at the moment.

It was about a month after Jean-Claude's return to Mali, however, that something developed which demanded that she actually suppress or sidetrack these irritating memories. She missed a period and began experiencing occasional nausea. For a desperate couple of days, she thought Jean-Claude had passed on to her some condition he had picked up in his workplace, and she resolved to go to a doctor and find out exactly what the problem was, mostly to still her fervent imagination and not have any unpleasant surprises to pass on to Jean-Claude.

The doctor had no doubt about it at all; she was pregnant. In this respect, Chloe had no memories to dredge up; she had always been scrupulously careful in this respect, having determined to herself that no accidents would happen which might have the potential to put her in an awkward or embarrassing situation. She had only ever had full sexual intercourse three times, and each case had been more about curiosity or a very occasional unanswerable lust, though the men who did that for her were very few and far between.

When she and Jean-Claude had first started making love, Chloe realised clearly enough that this was something she had done before, but never with someone as gentle and practised as Jean-Claude, who had clearly been a frequent lover before the loss of his wife, Madeleine.

Having discovered her pregnancy, Chloe was so delighted that she began to resist even the vague attempts at enlivening her memory which she had been making. This was the consummation, the justification, of her relationship with Jean-Claude, and while she had never been a habitual believer in signs and omens, her pregnancy seemed so definite an affirmation of the new situation that the past retreated even further into obscurity. Her instincts told her that she had never had children before, because the way it was making her feel, both mentally and physically, was certainly a new experience; whatever had caused the wiping of her memory, she felt certain that a pregnancy would be something she would not be able to forget, both in the experience and the consequences of it.

And her delight was intensified when Jean-Claude came home for his second leave, with six months of his contract already completed, and showed himself to be as delighted as she was. He and Madeleine, he related over one generously wine-sipping evening, had put off and put off attempting to have a child because of career considerations, until eventually time ran out when Madeleine fell ill and was no longer able to conceive.

He also had good news of his own. He had been putting out feelers in a few medical institutions in or near Marseilles, aided by the influence of his consultant friend Charles, and several possibilities were already looking promising.

Once more, he returned to Mali, and Chloe decided to join a pre-natal group of young mothers, which not only provided her with a few local friendships, but also led her into employment, helping out for a few hours a week at a local nursery. It was a very casual arrangement, all done by cash, without the need for any documentation or bureaucracy, as Chloe had already realised the French predilection for both and her own scanty records of a past which remained largely obscured.

She decided not to tell Jean-Claude until she could tell him to his face, and when he returned again, for a slightly longer leave of almost three weeks, she gave him her news and he gave her his. Hers seemed to give him an instant and much-needed boost, because once again, he returned looking pale and tired, his weariness seeming, to her, beyond even what might be expected from a long and mostly hot journey. However, he told her with some satisfaction that he now had only nine months left of his contract; he had been offered a post as a hospital doctor in the outskirts of Marseilles, thanks at least partly to the support of Charles and the backing of Médecins Sans Frontières.

'MSF are aware now that I am coming to the end of my useful service with them, Jeannette,' he said, having taken to his bed and remained there for four hours after getting home. 'They are not going to stand in my way if I take up the hospital job a little before my contract would have come to an end.'

The longer leave allowed him to recover most of his strength, and he was delighted that there was now the prospect of the Menteaus becoming a real family. He asked Chloe a lot of very professional questions regarding the progress of her pregnancy, and she had to remind herself that he was a doctor, unfamiliar as she was with men knowing such details.

But, of course, the inevitable question had to come, and it came when they were relaxing in a small restaurant which was becoming one of Chloe's favourites in Le Panier, as it provided private booths where it was possible to enjoy a confidential conversation as well as the superb food.

'Have you remembered anything else, Jeannette?' Jean-Claude asked.

At first, she tried to wave the question away; whatever that other life was still seemed so distant and remote, hardly worth disturbing their intimate moments.

'Our child, my darling,' he said, 'is going to be full of questions, as children always are. And they are also notoriously impatient with being fobbed off. When the other kids talk about their uncles and aunts, their grandads and grandmas, what will our son or daughter have to say? You've already mentioned that you have flickers and shadows, I think you called them. As and when things come back to you, Jeannette, we are going to have to deal with it. Trying to run away from your past altogether is a difficult business, to put it mildly. I still mentally see Madeleine sometimes, and when I'm working and things are becoming so hectic that I wonder whether I'll get through the day, I can sometimes hear her voice. She suggested to me once that she thought it might be a good idea for me to work for MSF for a while, and that's what partly decided me to go ahead and do it after she died.'

Chloe realised that Madeleine had to be added to her own flickers and shadows now; even though she had never known the woman, her influence was another piece in the growingly complicated jigsaw of her past existence.

'My mother was, and probably still is, a French woman,' she said hesitantly. 'I think my mother is the reason why I'm able to speak French in the first place. But my father is of a different nationality, and I suspect he is probably English. But who they are, and what they do, and even what they look like, is still mostly a mist to me.'

'The mist will clear, Jeannette, I'm sure. In the meantime, it is our child we must concentrate on. Perhaps my priorities are getting confused with this movement between France and Mali. But it won't be for much longer now.'

As the months passed, Chloe became more and more concerned with her child than anything else, and even when flickers of memory came to her, she tended to brush them away impatiently. The present and future had to take precedence over the past, for the moment at least.

Eighteen months after she disappeared from the Manningham Corporation, Chloe gave birth to a healthy and hefty boy. The fact that the child was a boy had become clear in an anatomy scan ultrasound in week twenty-two, and his name, Davide, had already been chosen. Davide Menteau was born in a Marseilles hospital while his father was doing his last working stint in Mali. The hospital agreed to send an urgent message to the camp where Jean-Claude was working, and the joyous return message caused everyone great pleasure.

Her baby was perfect, she was told; everything was in good working order, and the child began to demonstrate the power of his lungs within minutes of appearing. Chloe was up and moving about within hours of the birth, wishing fervently that her husband could be with her and telling anyone who had time to listen how wonderful it was to be a mother.

It was a little bit later, several days after the birth, that Chloe settling in at home with little Davide corresponded to a much more fraught and painful meeting taking place at Houghton Hall. Ralph and Brigitte Manningham were having a sombre meeting with their investigator, Sam Key, and a senior police officer, Superintendent George Rowan, of Brigitte's acquaintance. During Brigitte's days as a French politician, she had met Rowan a few times as he had the job of organising security for visiting European politicians, in order to avoid any diplomatic embarrassments for the British Government, even if his job was tied up with elaborate descriptions of international collaboration strategies.

'I wish, more than I can say, that I had something more definite to tell you, or at least a few leads to mention which we could take forward,' said Sam, and his unhappy appearance suggested that he felt his failure quite deeply. 'I cannot even establish beyond all reasonable doubt where Chloe went to after she landed at the airfield in Normandy. There are really only two feasible possibilities in relation to the airfield, and we have looked in detail at both of them, questioning the taxi drivers who habitually go to them, but without success. We know a few of them will say no anyway; they don't want to get involved at all with the British police. And, as you know, there is no guarantee that Chloe went wherever she went by taxi in the first place. We know that she speaks French very well, and buses would have been available to go to various places. The most likely place to go, given where she landed, would be Paris, of course, but you have mentioned, Lady Manningham, the various people you know in Paris and the Île-de-France, and from what you've told me, Chloe would have met quite a number of them herself.

'If she did go to the Paris area, there are thousands of hotels in that city, and of course, we don't know for certain that she went to a hotel. I know you have exhausted your contacts trying to find if she is with any one of them, Mrs. Manningham, and so far, drawn a blank. Everywhere, it seems, is a blank at the moment. I will carry on, of course, if you wish me to, and I gather Superintendent Rowan may have a few words of encouragement for you.'

'Yes, I think that's a fair statement, Mr. Key; not very much encouragement, perhaps, but some.' Rowan was a very large, military-looking figure, immaculate in his uniform, with a confidential manner born of keeping a lot of people's secrets as part of his daily work.

'The main consolation we can take from this at the moment, I think, is that Ms. Manningham has not disappeared in a Third World country, when almost anything could have happened. Had she been involved in a traffic accident, we would be able to gain access to the details, as all such incidents are recorded; we can say with some certainty that that has not happened. Had she been assaulted – forgive me, but we must eliminate the possibilities if we are going to get to the probabilities – that also would have shown up somewhere in police or court records. Her getting lost is an unlikely scenario, given that she is familiar with the territory and a fluent French speaker. My own theory, for what it's worth, is that she has gone to someone she knows, probably but not certainly in France, and someone she has met before in the course of her job. From what you've told me, Sir Ralph, she left after a particularly painful confrontation with a senior member of staff in the Manningham Corporation. She has perhaps decided that she needs to speak to some old friend, or just go to see a place she is familiar with from the past, so as to get her bearings. It is careless and inconsiderate of her to not let someone, and especially her parents, know where she is, but if she is highly stressed and uncertain of her future, the niceties might temporarily go out of the window.'

No members of his audience seemed very comforted by what he had said. Ralph Manningham in particular looked pale and stressed; he seemed still to be largely blaming himself for his daughter's disappearance. For a while, he sat staring at nothing in particular, with many fears and anxieties crowding in on his mind at once, and then he looked up to see that the other three people sitting dwarfed by the splendour of the main Houghton Hall living room were all looking at him, apparently expecting him to say something.

'Many thanks to both of you, gentlemen. The generations of my family seem fated to find themselves dealing with apparently insoluble conflicts. I had some very fundamental disagreements with my own father concerning the direction and development of the Manningham enterprise; being young, I was quite sure, beyond all doubt, that I was right, and he was wrong. Looking back on how it developed, I can see that there was a tenable case on both sides. Chloe and I have had serious differences ever since I decided she should become involved with the corporation at a very senior level; given her achievements and qualifications, I could hardly do anything else. Now the dispute I had with my father seems to have turned itself on its head. In those days, I was the progressive, the champion of the future, the one charged with moving the business on to more modern grounds; he was determined on the old ways, the value of tradition, the need for continuity above all. As if time wants to mock me for my presumption, now my daughter seeks to keep the whole enterprise on solid terra firma, not allowing for any attempts to move beyond planet Earth.'

The two men were beginning to show signs of restlessness, and Brigitte, even allowing for her expression of sympathy towards her husband, felt their awkwardness.

'That's all true and generally relevant, darling, but these gentlemen are busy people and I think we need to stick to the immediate practicalities.'

For a moment, Ralph stared intensely at her, as if she had uttered a blasphemy. Then he remembered himself and where he was.

'Yes, of course. I was trying to sketch out background, but I take the point. We must seek to decide what we can do next. Is there anything still to be done, or do we simply wait?'

Sam was the first to accept the challenge.

'As long as you want me to, Sir Ralph, I will keep looking. I've found even more obscure needles in even bigger haystacks, but this one is particularly intractable. However, as the superintendent says, we do have a few leads, vague as they may be, and we can rule out a few things with a fair degree of confidence. Alerts have already been put out to all French airports, and I do think that if Chloe had tried to leave the country, we would probably know about it. She is somewhere in France, and hopeless as that might sound in relation to such a huge country, it does offer possibilities in terms of circulating to the SNCF rail stations, the local hospitals and the regional police stations. All is far from lost.'

'Absolutely,' chimed in the superintendent, with a heartiness which didn't fool either of the worldly Manningham parents. But, for the moment, their only available currency was hope and a refusal to countenance the more horrendous possibilities.

When the policeman and the private investigator had gone, the Manninghams held each other closely for some time. The physical side of their relationship had faded from the great passion of its early days, but there was still reassurance and strength to be drawn from each other, even as their nightmare continued.

PART THREE

AWAKENING

The days after taking Davide home were some of the most joyous Chloe could remember in her life and seemed to justify all the faith and effort she had put into her new life. Jean-Claude now only had a relatively short three-month stretch to do before his service with MSF was over, and then they could, at last, begin to live properly as a united family, with no more digressions or distractions to deal with. Chloe began to think that she might be able to do more in the childcare field as Davide grew older, and supplement Jean-Claude's earnings at the hospital with an income of her own.

Davide had been home for nearly a month when Jean-Claude returned for his last ever leave. For a while, he simply sat silently holding the baby, with tears quietly running down his cheeks. In the previous week, two babies had died in his arms of conditions too far gone for any medication to save them. This was his son, his very own son, and he was immensely, fervently grateful, even if the contrast between the situation of little Davide Menteau could not contrast more markedly with the desperation of two tiny African babies.

But, for once, he left to return to Mali with a feeling of optimism and fulfilment, knowing the promise of a family life before him when he returned, as well as a professional environment where the job did not have to be undermined so constantly by negative factors which he could do nothing about.

A few weeks after he left, Chloe's mood began to change, and even though she knew that some post-natal reaction had always been a possibility, it was difficult for her to easily deal with it. Davide was noisy and constantly demanding, and no one was there to deal with his demands, day or night, but her. That was only to be expected. What was not expected to the same extent, even though it was at least as problematic, was the growing return of her memory.

She recognised that she had been so obsessed with her pregnancy and ensuring a safe birth that she had thrust everything else away into the darker recesses of her mind. And now, the memories were demanding release with every bit as much energy and determination as Davide called for her attention.

She was sitting near a children's playground not far from the centre of Marseilles one day, when a sudden, overwhelming flood descended on her. Davide was, of course, still too young to use any of the playground equipment, but she liked to come to this place and think of when he would be able to do so.

Suddenly, her surroundings began to remind her of somewhere else entirely, and the vision shouted at her of the exact spot in Paris where she had met Jean-Claude. She had remembered their first meeting before, but the difference this time was she could also place where she had come from that morning. With a bizarre mixture of revelation and depression, she could even remember the name of the hotel.

For several hours to follow, her mind was racing. She could trace back the whole adventure which had led her to that bench in the Place Vendôme and her meeting with Jean-Claude. She had flown into France on a little plane, and her memory was suggesting to her that it was her own plane, flown by an employee of her own company. Because she had been to that airfield before, she knew exactly how and where she could get a taxi to take her into Paris, and the hotel she had pre-booked.

But tantalisingly, she still could not remember her name, or where she had come from, or what she was doing travelling to Paris in the first place.

Davide was crying in his pram and some woman at the children's playground was looking at her with something approaching censure and disapproval. A finger sign came to her mind, a very rude finger sign, although it was not a French gesture, and the woman probably wouldn't understand it. So whose gesture was it? Where had she been flying from? If Jean-Claude was right about her English accent, it had to be from England.

By the time she had got Davide home and fed him, the need to go to Paris and track down that hotel had impressed itself forcefully on her. For once, Davide settled down to a nap after his feed without a lot of bother, and she could turn her mind to determining what exactly to do next. She had made a few friends at the nursery, and she knew she could safely leave Davide with them for a day. Phoning the Paris hotel would not do; she knew how off-hand the Parisians could be, and the chances were that they would deny any memory of it rather than have to bother themselves with trying to remember. She wrote down the name of the hotel so that she wouldn't forget it again.

A whisper at the back of her mind urged her to forget the whole thing and simply embrace her new life and everything in it. But she knew it was already too late – the fog had lifted, and now there was a growing urgency in her to discover everything she had been, because if she didn't, the aching curiosity would never go away. With a realisation which was almost the mental equivalent of a hard slap in the face, it occurred to her at last that there might well be people in her old world, wherever and whatever it was, who had been going out of their mind with worry about where she was and what had happened to her.

A little research told her that she could fly to Paris and back on the same day for a reasonable sum of money. She had some money of her own, partly from her earnings and partly from what Jean-Claude had gifted her, and when she realised that the whole trip was logistically perfectly feasible, she felt a growing excitement at the possibility of what she might be able to discover.

Several days later, with Davide safely installed at the nursery and arrangements made with a good friend to take care of him after the nursery closed if she wasn't back in time, she flew to Paris. She had researched online as to where the hotel was, and she tracked the connections down after arriving at the Gare du Nord.

At the hotel, she found herself talking to a heavily made-up, bored-looking young lady in an odd air hostess-like uniform at the reception desk. The woman seemed either unable or unwilling to understand exactly what was being asked of her, and eventually Chloe demanded to see someone in a higher managerial position.

A middle-aged man, clearly a little irritated at having been distracted from whatever it was he had been doing, arrived at the desk.

'I stayed here some time ago, *monsieur*, and for reasons which I really don't need to bother you with, I absent-mindedly left some belongings at this hotel. I am not trying to get anything refunded, as your young lady here seemed to think; I am simply trying to locate what I left here.'

'I see. And when would this have been, *madame*?'

Chloe had done her best to trace back the exact date, but she could not get closer than a five-day period. The man sighed extravagantly, and then took some keys from his pocket.

'Perhaps you will come with me, *madame*?'

Some distance behind the reception desk, in a small passage which appeared to be leading out to a car park, the man unlocked a room which consisted almost entirely of four shelves containing bags and cases of all shapes and sizes.

'These are the various objects which have been left with us in recent years. We do have tourists visiting us from a large variety of places. For the period of time you describe, *madame*, whatever we have will probably be somewhere in the furthest shelf away from you here. You are welcome to try and locate it there if you wish.'

Chloe looked at the shelf he indicated and sighed equally heavily in her turn. She didn't hold out much hope, but she knew she had to try. As it happened, she was lucky; not more than ten minutes into the search, she recognised a handsome little leather bag which she sometimes used as a shoulder bag and sometimes as a handbag. Almost immediately underneath it was the economical little mauve suitcase she knew she used for what were planned to be fairly short trips.

In the bag was her passport and a moderate sum in euros. She almost broke down in tears when she looked at the passport and saw her picture, not a bad one by passport standards, and her name – Chloe Manningham.

The man was still at the reception desk when she returned.

'So,' he said, seeming to force a grin onto his face, 'you are claiming this bag, *madame*. Can you show us whether there is anything in it which specifically identifies it as yours?'

Chloe showed him the passport, and he seemed satisfied. Chloe's incredulity forced her to ask him a question.

'Did it not occur to you, *monsieur*, to report this to the gendarmes?'

He actually laughed, briefly, and even the air-hostess girl permitted herself a wan smile.

'If we went to the gendarmerie, *madame*, with everything which is left with us, we would have very little time for anything else. We are not a lost-property agency. We keep everything for a generous period, to allow whoever left their possessions here to claim them, as you have just done. I think that is all that can be expected of us.'

Chloe realised that the hotel had done for her all that they were going to do and took her belongings to a nearby café in order to check them all through.

Now the discovery had been made, she had to think through the ramifications of it carefully. She still wasn't entirely sure who

Chloe Manningham was, or why she had been travelling to Paris. And the realisation that something had happened of sufficient impact and importance to temporarily wipe her memory away was intimidating in itself. Who or what could cause such a thing?

For a few wild moments, she actually contemplated not returning to Marseilles at all. She had been living in a dream; her whole French existence, her marriage, her child were all parts of a gigantic fantasy. But she could remember Jean-Claude clearly enough; the scent of him, his spare, muscular body, his deep eyes which could reveal or hide as he chose, his obvious passion for her, and his constant kindness. Her husband was real, immediate and no fantasy, and so was her son, a child too young and innocent to have to suffer the consequences of whatever nonsenses his mother had contrived to do with her life. And she knew now that it was Jean-Claude, and only him, who had managed to overcome her doubts and reticence about having any children at all.

Parts of her former life were now drifting back to her, like the bits and pieces of a language once learnt and since obscured from her mind. And, at last, the shadowy mystery of the man overwhelmingly in her former life, who could only be her father, was clarifying, slowly but surely.

She took comfort from the knowledge and opportunity that finding her bag had restored to her. Everywhere she looked at the moment seemed to be a wild, tangled mess, but now at least she had the means to start putting things back into a coherent shape. For so long, life seemed to be doing whatever it chose to do with her, without her being able to assert herself and move things away from seemingly inexorable and inevitable directions. But the voice she was rediscovering told her that she had never previously been used to being a victim of life, unable to go anywhere but where the wind blew her. She needed to regain control and make her own decisions on where next to go.

Yes, she would return to Marseilles; that much was inevitable, for the moment at least. She would see how Jean-Claude would react to these new developments, and what kind of regime was going to be put in place when Jean-Claude had finally finished his service in Mali. Being a married woman with a young child, and perhaps more children to follow, if that's what she and her husband decided on, might be enough; it might be the life she had always coveted, very domestic, very firmly based, and with the prospect of watching the children grow and make their own way in the world. It might be enough, but somehow, she doubted it. Whatever was still lurking in her past life for her to rediscover, she strongly suspected that she had had broader horizons and bigger issues to deal with, that she had a different take on the business of everyday life which an existence of simple domesticity would not satisfy.

One woman had travelled from Marseilles to Paris, but two women returned, and even during the course of the journey, Chloe Manningham was announcing her restoration with increasing emphasis. And so, more and more, was Ralph Manningham, so that, by the time her train moved in to Marseilles station, she knew who he was, what he meant to her, and what she had probably recently done to his life.

Several weeks later, Jean-Claude returned to Marseilles to take up a job at home. His relief and joy was all too abundantly obvious, and initially, Chloe downplayed the extent of her memory's recovery. His pleasure was infectious, and there was no avoiding the extra convenience of him being at home. She realised how lonely and self-obsessed she had tended to become during his long absences, and for a while, she tried almost desperately to simply adjust to her domestic life.

Less than two months into their reunited married life, the crunch came quite suddenly and more emphatically than either of them could easily cope with. Chloe had been taking precautions to avoid another pregnancy, and Jean-Claude had accepted that, realising that she did not want to go through the experience again so soon. But, inevitably, the issue of whether they should have another child to join Davide came up. Jean-Claude now had a better-paid job than his post with MSF, and he was committed to staying where he was for the foreseeable future.

'It's time now, Jeannette, isn't it? I don't think we ever had it in mind for Davide to be an only child, did we?'

They were sitting in the compact back garden of their Marseilles house, its high walls affording them a reasonable measure of privacy, though the fact that it was located in a city was all too obvious from the sounds and odours around them.

Chloe had, at that moment, been thinking again about her parents, and in particular her mother, who had spent so much time and effort acting as a referee and go-between for the endless disagreements with her father. Brigitte, she knew very well, had done nothing at all to deserve the disappearance of her daughter; nothing could be said or done to justify the way she had treated her mother, even if it was accidental and never meant.

'My name is Chloe, Jean-Claude; I cannot maintain the pretence of another name any longer. Neither can I contemplate another child until the tangled mess of my past is sorted out, or at the least better dealt with than it has been so far.'

'I see.' She could also see, clearly enough, the pain in his eyes, that the domestic life he had been looking forward to for so long was now so seriously compromised. She could also hear the tears in his voice. It seemed that, whichever way she turned, someone would finish up getting hurt.

He seemed to be making an effort to resign himself to something, and she felt the situation was already spiralling out of the control of either of them. The way his eyes followed her movements now suggested that both he and the woman he could truly believe was anyone else but his wife, seemed to have moved beyond the range of conciliation and compromise.

However, his words eventually belied what his eyes appeared to be saying.

'I suppose we both knew this was going to happen sooner or later. I don't want to share a life with you if you feel that it is somehow a lie. Perhaps it would be best for you to go back to England and understand what it was that caused you to lose your memory so completely, although I have to say, Jeannette or Chloe, whoever you want to be, that if it was something hurtful and traumatic enough to deprive you of your memory, you must realise that you are taking a considerable risk in returning to it.'

Chloe looked at him for some time, and one memory did return very powerfully; his calm, handsome face gazing at her across the Place Vendôme when her entire world seemed to have crashed around her. Somehow, she had to make him understand.

'Jean-Claude. Dear, darling Jean Claude. I already know of two people who are gigantic figures in my past; my mother and my father. As far as my memory has recovered of whatever it was that caused my flight to France, it had a lot to do with my differences with my father on what the Manningham Corporation should be and do. But those differences don't mean that I hated him, or he hated me; quite the opposite, in fact, because if I didn't love him and admire him, if I hadn't grown up cherishing his great intelligence and ability, I would never have taken some rift with him so very seriously. I still can't remember what it was we differed about, though I do know it was something absolutely fundamental to the future of the Manningham project. I know that in his past he had a serious difference of opinion with his own father, and he eventually decided to go his own way, even to the extent of replacing his own father as the effective head of the organisation. Maybe I have been somehow destined to go the same way. How many of us do finish up finding ourselves defying, or even fighting against, the aims and wishes of our parents? And at a time when technological progress is so bewilderingly fast, how can we not?

They champion the world they have known; we know that world has changed and moved on, and now, inevitably, there are different rules and objectives. But however I disagree with him, I can't just walk away from him and leave him thinking I have died, and possibly died because some intransigence of his has destroyed my mind. Whatever he is or ever was, he has done nothing to deserve that. And if my memory has so betrayed me, it's because of my love and respect for him, not because I want to expunge him from my life for ever. I have to go back to England and make things as right as possible, Jean-Claude, or I shall never be able to regain my peace of mind at all.'

For what seemed like a long time, Jean-Claude simply gazed at his wife. In his mind, endless combinations of words were presenting themselves, as he tried to find some way of defending his family and his happiness. He had told himself repeatedly that this moment was always going to come sooner or later, but he had somehow remained hoping that it would be an abusive husband, or some trauma involving members of a constantly quarrelsome family, which had given rise to his wife's amnesia – something so bad that she had determined to leave it all behind her and start again, so that her mind had interpreted her wishes and obliged accordingly.

Now, it seemed as if it had actually been a type of intellectual overload; that Chloe, who in the normal way of her life aspired to great heights of scientific and administrative experience, had blown some kind of mental fuse, and perhaps all that was then wanted was a total change of scene and atmosphere, causing her to revert to the easy domesticity which had never previously held much attraction for her.

'Whatever your father was or is, my darling, you finished up in France largely as a result of your French mother, meaning in the middle of your crisis, it was your mother and your Frenchness which your mind decided would provide you with some shelter and a framework for recovery. You found the alternative, and it was maybe the alternative you have always secretly coveted. It's almost as if masculinity and femininity have been turned on their head. How many men, over the years, have had to believe that the aim of their life was to rise as far as possible in whatever hierarchy occupied their working days, because that was the pressure continuously exerted on them by everyone else's expectations, when all they really wanted was to live a fairly easy, pedestrian life, a simple domestic set-up where they could do what they had to do during the day and then go home to the wife and the kids?

'I have something of that in myself. I started with MSF wanting to go all the way, to finish up controlling what was happening rather than just contributing my modest effort to it while others ran the show. Then I found the heat, the relentlessness, the agonising choices which all doctors need to make in such circumstances, were slowly grinding me down. Ambitious career plans have to come up against the brutal realities, sooner or later, of your own limitations. Over the years, I suppose countless men have come up against this, but women in previous generations, who didn't have the career choices open to them in the first place, were always left with unanswered questions on what they really could or could not do.

'Did you really want to regard the job in your father's company as the pinnacle of your ambition, and if you didn't, what would, or could you do about it? Did he ever ask you directly whether you really wanted to do the jobs he had in mind for you? You fled to France, my darling Jeannette, because that is who you are to me, to get away from a life which was putting more pressure on you than your mind or your memory could tolerate. And you think the cure for that is to go straight back to it and try again? It doesn't make sense. Yes, sure, tell your mother and father you're alive and well, put them out of their worry and suffering about that, but then, the best thing to do is return to the new life which you worked out for yourself to save you from the problems of the old. Tell your mother and father that here in Marseilles is where you want to be, with your husband and child, and then they can come and visit whenever they choose, as can anybody else in your family you miss and want to see again. All of us only have one life, Jeannette. It doesn't make sense to waste it trying to be something we're not.'

At this point, Davide decided to make his presence emphatically felt, and the routine of the day took over from the disputed issues of the future. But Chloe continued to struggle with deciding what to do next, and even though Jean-Claude had made clear that he had no objection to her going back to England to meet and reassure her parents, Chloe felt that such a trip might force her into the rejection of one life or the other, because it would make only too clear the impossibility of continuing with both simultaneously. And she had come to accept that even if she did temporarily decide on a life of pure domesticity in France, it probably would not be enough for her in the future, particularly if it included having and bringing up more children.

So days turned to weeks, and still she made no definite commitment to one life or the other. During this period, another difficult encounter was taking place between her parents, as they sought to deal with her continued non-appearance.

This time, the background to their conversation was not the relatively domestic surroundings of Houghton Hall, but the top-floor chairman's office of the Manningham Corporation in London.

Ralph had just abruptly rejected yet another journalistic approach for comments or "perspectives" on how management affairs at the corporation were likely to change now that the chief executive was no longer in office, which he rightly saw as yet another angle on his daughter's disappearance. Brigitte was making another of her now more frequent visits to London, as she sought to get whatever help she could from her political connections, in both Britain and France. By now, both of them were weary and frustrated with the whole business, and their anxiety for their daughter was mingling with their sense of infuriated indignation that she had subjected them to such an ordeal in the first place. Brigitte was sitting on the chair in front of her husband's desk, in the kind of position where she might be about to be interviewed for a job, and had circumstances been different, both of them would have derived some amusement from the situation, but one look at Brigitte's unhappy, bewildered expression made clear enough that nothing else was influencing them at the moment but anxiety and insecurity.

'I have to think that something must have happened to her, Ralph. I simply can't believe that she would voluntarily subject us to this; it goes against everything I've ever known about her. She can be some negative things, I know, but to leave us hanging in the void like this, day after day, week after week; such a deliberate act would be the mark of a sadist, or someone who felt she had an elaborate score to settle, and she's never given me that impression. I know the two of you have had your differences, and I'm not underestimating how serious those differences have sometimes been. The ultimate direction of the company, and its efforts to move itself in the right direction, is serious enough, but when she has opinions on that subject, she will say so loud and clear.'

'Yes, I know that well enough. I've been here in this office arguing with her on a number of occasions now, and she puts across her point of view, usually very directly and emphatically. She's fond of talking about the Manningham Corporation's "social responsibilities", though she never seems quite so concerned about the simple question of whether the corporation is making enough money to survive. It reminds me sometimes of the kind of arguments I used to have with my father. "Look, Ralph," he'd say, "a lot of my workforce" – he always talked like that, as though they were his personal possession – "have been with us for years; they're used to working in certain ways, and they're used to producing the goods that this company has made famous – we're a household name, son. You seem to be asking that we throw all that away. Where does that leave them, the people who've made this firm?".

"It will probably leave them unemployed, Dad," I would say to him. You've got to make stuff that suits the time you live in, otherwise what you're making becomes obsolete. You can have all the pure and idealistic business aims you like, but if you don't make any money, you go bust, and then no one has a job, traditional or otherwise. Chloe is able, imaginative and highly intelligent, but she has the same sort of blinkers on. "We need to do something to help this planet, Dad, before we go tinkering about in others". So, OK, great, Chloe, I say, but how does going into Third World countries to help with their agricultural, transport and building problems actually make us money rather than cost us a hell of a lot? We need projects which will enthuse people, wealthy people, and national governments, for that matter. We need ideas which will advance technology, like all the benefits which followed from the moon landings all those years ago. We need the help of good publicity, and even intelligent sponsorship, which is not a dirty word—'

'Yes, Ralph, I know the arguments, both yours and hers. I have heard them many times. I'm not sure how going over them all again is going to help with the situation we're facing at the moment. I feel an absolute imperative to do something, but I don't know what. If nothing presents itself, we have no choice left but to accept that Chloe is—'

Ralph suddenly burst out of his chair and went to the window to look down at the teeming city below. Brigitte guessed he was trying to hide the tears in his eyes and wondered why she seemed to have none of her own as yet. Had he, who thought of himself as the ultimate realist, finally accepted that his daughter had died? And if so, why couldn't she?

'Chloe is widely known, in this country at least, even if she isn't a film star or a politician. I just can't come to terms with her disappearing so totally. Even if she was on the continent, there could well be English people holidaying or working there who might recognise her, or people from other companies who might know her from conferences or news reports. If there has been a road accident, or an aircraft accident, or even an attack on her by some lunatic or someone with terrorist ideas—'

'Please don't, Brigitte,' said her husband's voice quietly from the window.

'We must face facts, Ralph. She has disappeared into thin air, and we have to look at the grimmer possibilities now if we are to have any chance of finding her—'

'She's dead, Brigitte. That's the reality of this. That's the fact we have to face.'

He turned back towards her, not bothering to try to disguise the anguish on his face.

'I don't know how. An attack down some deserted country lane. A car crash which left her unrecognisable. Perhaps even an innocent swimming escapade – you know well enough how impulsive she is. Or some kind of experiment with drink or drugs. How much do we know of her private life, when all's said and done? She's never had a boyfriend for any length of time, she's never been anywhere near marrying anyone – what do we really know about how she likes to amuse herself, and who she likes to amuse herself with?'

'No more, Ralph, please.'

Ralph sat down again to see the tears running down his wife's face. Oddly, he found himself trying to remember the last time he had seen her like this, and he realised very rapidly that he never had seen her like this. Perhaps this, more than anything else, was the most unforgivable part of his daughter's disappearance.

He watched Brigitte as she cried, with no attempt to disguise or control what she was doing, and he could not deny to himself that he had wanted to do exactly the same thing himself at the moment when he walked to the window, but somehow, he simply couldn't. Maybe that was another legacy from his father, who regarded displays of emotion from men, or even from boys, as out of order and socially embarrassing. He knew a dam was building inside him which could well have some devastating consequences if it couldn't find some form of release soon. The death of his daughter, because that was what he had to acknowledge to himself now was almost certainly the case, was a crippling blow to his entire life's work. There were men, he knew well enough, who would be unable to see their visions of the future entirely embodied in a daughter. Her children would almost certainly not bear his surname, and many fathers would point to the distractions of marriage and childbirth as convincing reasons why they could not fully embrace their daughters as heirs.

But Chloe, he had always felt, was different. She had not only the intellectual but the sheer physical capacity to be a leading standard bearer for her family. Whoever she married, if she ever did marry, would have to work with her rather than over her, and if she was placed in a very senior position in the company, the likelihood of anyone, male or female, questioning such an appointment would be very low.

Now, it seemed that he had to find a chief executive again or return to doing the job himself. He wanted to do neither of these and he felt a certain pang of self-contempt when he realised that he was grieving as much for the consequences of his daughter's disappearance as he was for Chloe herself. He could appoint an energetic yes-man; there would be no shortage of candidates who could fit that bill.

But he knew that there were many people in his business, both inside and outside Manningham Corporation, who would tend to agree with Chloe. To move so much in the way of resources, material and intellectual, to concentrating on developing living space away from planet Earth meant that the chances of rescuing the planet from its ultimate dire fate became even slimmer. When would the population finally come to realise that the game was up, and what would they then do? Perhaps the real impetus behind Chloe's ideas was something similar to a faithful servant trying to hold back her blind master before he plunged headlong over the cliff side, into a world of abandoned anarchy, where no further rules existed except survival of the fittest and all remaining human civilisation gave way to the laws of the jungle.

As he sat slumped in his big managerial chair, listening to his wife's cries slowly subsiding into silence, Ralph felt once again the pains in his chest which were becoming an all too familiar part of his daily routine, and as usual, he lined up the defences of his various forms of dismissal; indigestion, a result of his varied and unpredictable diet; some kind of respiratory difficulties resulting from the cold he had had a few weeks ago, or perhaps just a consequence of the fact that he was ageing, as everybody did. The pain persisted and intensified, but Ralph concentrated on making it go away, and eventually, it did. *All to the good*, he thought; *I have more serious things to worry about.*

Just over three weeks after this incident in the main Manningham office, Chloe finally came to an irrevocable decision. She knew Jean-Claude would not like it. She knew she might well be parachuting herself back into the tortured situation which had caused her crisis in the first place, but she knew also that she had been prevaricating for far too long and the consequences of that would by now be deeply felt by her parents. Jean-Claude had cooled on her ever since his return from Mali. He had returned to a life of domestic bliss, as he saw it, finally free of all the privations of Third World existence. He would work in a hospital not constantly running out of equipment and resources and live in a society where the ever-present menace of fanatical supposedly religious maniacs did not hang over so many aspects of everyday life. He would grow his family with his remarkable English wife and see her enjoying her continuing release from the convoluted crisis that her former life had become.

But that is not what had happened. His wife now had almost total recall of her former circumstances, and instead of being grateful for the escape which her failed memory had provided for her, she felt a seemingly compulsive urge to go back and disentangle what she had so clearly been unable to disentangle before. She had refused his repeated pleas for them to attempt to procreate a brother or sister for Davide, and the outgoing, sociable Chloe he had known had become introverted and preoccupied as she tried to make herself accommodate her changed circumstances.

Eventually, and grudgingly, as they both sat in a comfortable café in central Marseilles, Jean-Claude tried to think of ways to make the situation more palatable.

'At least use your passport as my wife,' he said. 'God only knows what the British press have been doing with the story of your disappearance. It's quite possible that people might still be watching docks and airports to see if anyone of your name enters the country. You could find yourself in a police station being interrogated before you ever get to see your parents. Go into the country as Jeannette Menteau, a casual tourist. That will give you time to think about what you want to do and where you want to go, without people stopping your mission before it ever gets started.'

Chloe could see clearly enough his reluctance to assist in what he saw as an essentially bad idea, but she knew her Jean-Claude pretty well by this time and she understood the way his mind worked. If something appeared to be inevitable, whether he liked it or not, he would do his best to think of how best it could be undertaken, an asset which she understood must have been essential for him in his MSF work. And what he said was true; suddenly appearing in Britain as Chloe Manningham could be disastrous for her if word got straight back to her parents that she was in the country and hadn't even notified them of her coming. She did think, long and hard, about contacting them before she made the trip, so that they could be at least reassured that she was still alive and well, but to give an explanation of everything which had happened to her over the phone, without any prior knowledge of where they might be or what they might be doing, was a daunting prospect. Her father, in particular, might instantly be demanding long explanations, and instead of the reconciliation she needed, she could find herself involved in a major row, causing things to be said on both sides which might take a lot of unsaying. When she was much closer to them, and about to appear at the hall, would be a better time to make the call.

And at that moment, she remembered Aitken's Wood, her refuge throughout childhood and adolescence. She had made it her domain; whoever came and stayed with her did so on her terms. It was where she had educated herself in many departments outside the school curriculum, not least the finding out about boys, both physically and mentally. Their importance to the present and future of her life had been obvious to her from the start, as had her refusal to believe that her half-brother Miles was necessarily a reliable example of the species generally. It hadn't taken her long to discover that the cliché often attached to them, of being obsessed with sexual activity and their own bodies, was true only of some of them, and even then, in widely diverse ways. She encountered boys who were, for one reason or the other, more or less indifferent to the subject, either because of simple immaturity or other preoccupations, and similarly, she knew others for whom the word obsession would not be inappropriate. These boys could be predatory or have an ambition in their minds to become so, and the various horror stories sometimes told about them by the girls could make further contact or sympathetic communication very difficult.

But mostly, her time at Aitken's Wood was about educating herself on the natural world, and living in an environment that was less cluttered and clamouring than her school or her home. The fact that her parents were both important people became firmly lodged in her mind at an early age. Houghton Hall was often full of people, and sometimes most of them were people she didn't know. Spending time alone with either of her parents ranged from difficult to well-nigh impossible, especially during the day. For most days, she was at school all day anyway, but even later on, her father would be constantly on the phone or talking to people in his study. She knew he wanted her to learn from him, and she did, in a number of ways, by observing him as well as talking to him, but the older she got, the more she found herself seeing clearly enough the differences between them, and while it seemed incredibly presumptuous of her to start doubting whether he was absolutely right on certain issues, the doubts couldn't help but develop into actual differences with him in time.

Aitken's Wood was just about the trees, the birds and the various other woodland creatures, along with whoever, male or female, she allowed to join her. Even though it was separated from the grounds of Houghton Hall, it was nevertheless part of the estate which came with the hall, meaning that only she and her half-brother and sister were actually entitled to be there, of all the kids she knew. Miles tended to have other concerns and seemed reluctant to move anywhere that wasn't in sight of Houghton Hall; Anne was more interested in clothes, make-up and food than she was in anything to do with the natural world. They also, she felt, resented her dominance when her friends were with her in the wood, and Anne was uncomfortable in the company of boys.

On occasions, with her parents' agreement, she had spent several days in the wood. In her younger days, her father would appoint someone to keep an eye on her, but they were generally instructed to keep their distance. At times, when they had something about them which Chloe liked, she might even involve them in some of her activities.

Yes, she decided, she would return to Aitken's Wood first, and allow herself to be there long enough to relax into that peaceful environment. She doubted whether anyone would be watching the wood now, and she knew enough about how to make herself comfortable there without being seen in any case.

On a bleak Monday morning, Chloe Manningham, alias Jeannette Menteau, flew into Manchester Airport. She had decided to avoid the London airports because of the increased possibility that someone might recognise her there.

Her heart was beating so rapidly as she went through the passport check that she was afraid the man checking them might hear it. But he looked casually at her passport, and then at her, and minutes later, she was walking back into her home country once again. She had arranged for a taxi to meet her and take her to an anonymous hotel in central Manchester, where she would spend a couple of nights, get her bearings, and decide her next move.

PART FOUR

RESOLUTION

Bellamy was back in his study, and in deep reflection again. Cases which appeared insoluble tended to have that effect on him, as if his inbuilt confidence had grown to the point where he determined that anything could eventually be solved as long as he thought long and hard enough about it.

He gazed at a print of a Hockney painting on his wall, taken from one of the paintings the artist had done of his Yorkshire homeland. It portrayed a long, receding avenue of trees, with the typical spellbinding vividness of colour associated with the painter, which even an inexpensive print could not fail to catch. The line didn't seem to lead anywhere but further woodland, onward apparently to infinity. It somehow seemed to reflect his emotions.

He had made a couple more trips to Houghton Hall in an attempt to keep the investigations alive, accompanied by Elaine, as always, though even Elaine was now showing signs of impatience at having to plug away at the Manningham case. The media had also largely lost interest; only a few young men and women, the press people who languished in positions only slightly above the tea boy or girl status, were sent to stand outside the hall just in case something of interest might happen.

The word had got round, as words tended to do, that Ralph Manningham had died of natural causes, and the police were trying to keep the case alive just to somehow justify their existence. The politicians, particularly those of the party which had received Manningham's donations, were becoming increasingly incensed that the case wasn't just being put to bed. Bellamy had had two further extremely terse phone conversations with Gregson, and even Tom Hollins was beginning to lose patience with his buddy's obstinacy.

Just to protect his back, Bellamy had spoken to the source of his offer to rejoin the journalistic world, and the offer had been both confirmed and underlined; the source had even added extra money to the pay being suggested. He knew he could resign safely in the sense of going straight into different employment as and when he felt he had to, but he also knew it would be with a sense of failure which might well accompany him to his new job, perhaps meaning a slide into mediocrity or increasing frustration.

His instinctive belief that Chloe Manningham was still alive had remained with him, and as far as he was concerned, it was based on simple logical deduction and reasoning. He had spoken extensively to those people closest to Chloe, and while some perspectives differed according to who he was talking to and their own particular relationships with her, the story remained remarkably consistent. The woman was highly intelligent, capable of making people do what she wanted them to do without them feeling bad about it, eloquent in describing her thoughts and feelings, certainly not easily manipulated, either by women or men, and able to hold down a highly demanding job which, even though it had been obtained as a result of her family connections, no one even suggested was a matter of nepotism and beyond her abilities.

Whatever had caused Chloe to leave the country – and it was by no means proved beyond reasonable doubt, as far as Bellamy was concerned, that she definitely had left the country – she would not have gone without some feasible means of keeping in contact with her work colleagues and her family. If sudden death had happened, which for an active woman of her age was highly unlikely unless someone else had caused it by violence or traffic accident, it was difficult, verging on impossible, to believe that there wouldn't have been some trace, some evidence of it. If someone had threatened or pursued her, she was more than savvy enough to get help or even deal with it herself.

Brigitte Manningham and her family were, of course, devastated, and loyal as Brigitte, a remarkable woman by anyone's standards, remained to the cause of establishing exactly what had happened, she had now lost her husband and her daughter, both in tragic and not adequately explained circumstances, and if she continued for much longer without some kind of closure, even the redoubtably tough Brigitte would be in deep psychological trouble which might have all sorts of consequences, none of them good.

The temptation to resign and use his new journalistic status to vent his spleen on politicians and police alike remained very strong, but it still, to Bellamy, most resembled moving away from his own mess to leave others to clean it up.

His mind was drifting towards trying another sweep of Brigitte's contacts and colleagues to try and get at least a sniff of a new line of enquiry. Chloe's disappearance had now become an even bigger mystery than the death of her father, but Bellamy felt that by now he had an intimate knowledge of both of them and still, deep in his gut where his most acute professional instincts remained positioned, he felt that the two incidences were connected.

A car was approaching. Bellamy lived in a largely rural area, away from the clatter of traffic and city life generally, and the approach of a motor vehicle was clear enough. The car would only be heading for Bellamy's house if the noise reached a certain volume, and when it did, he allowed his reverie to recede and went to the window to see who it might be.

It was clearly Elaine, and in normal circumstances, that would set off at least a tiny frisson of excitement in him about what might have happened to bring her to him when a visit from her had not been scheduled, but now he felt it would almost certainly mean more obfuscation and frustration for both of them, and the idea that it might be a mercy on his part to release her from this case was settling in his mind, until he saw the way she hurriedly parked the car and almost jumped out of it.

A minute later, after a brief and obviously amicable conversation with Louise downstairs, Elaine was with him. She held several pieces of paper in her hand.

'This, sir,' she said, selecting the paper on top of her pile, 'has come to us from a particularly intelligent and on-the-ball security guy at Manchester Airport. He took some footage of a young woman making her way through the airport, including when she stopped at passport check, because he had seen some circulated pictures of Chloe Manningham, and even though this woman came in under another name with a valid French passport, he says she is the spitting image of Chloe.'

By now, Bellamy had seen so many pictures and videos of Chloe Manningham that there was little chance of him not recognising her. The picture at passport check was particularly close and detailed.

'That lady,' he said, 'is Chloe Manningham, whatever she's calling herself. But hang on…'

He looked at the date below the picture.

'This is over a month ago.'

'Yes, sir. Our eagle-eyed guy had a bit of a job persuading his elders and betters that there was anything here they should be involving themselves in. They were leaning on him to forget it, and he had to go upstairs to get them to register how important it might be. Eventually, it got to a DCS, who checked it out and insisted it be sent on. Then it got to Tom Holl— I mean Detective Superintendent Hollins, sir, who sent it straight on.'

Bellamy was conscious of a long-standing ache, living in him like a dose of something unpleasant, slowly starting to ease. The photographs were undeniably of Chloe Manningham, and while the mystery remained as to why she should be flying into the country with a French passport, his instincts had nevertheless once again been proved right, and the faith in himself which, even after all this time, had started to shake just a little, was on its way to restoration.

'If you can fish out the name of that airport guy, Elaine, please let me know. I don't suppose he'd be too excited at the promise of a kiss from me, but something to help him along to his next promotion might be in order. Now we need to look at the airport CCTV and see if there are any clues about where she was going.'

'What about Mrs. Manningham, sir? Are we certain enough about the identification to tell her that Chloe is alive?'

Bellamy made a mental note of yet another example of Elaine's capacity to press the exactly relevant buttons in any particular situation, and his mind immediately turned to Brigitte's continued anguish. It was, in one particularly cruel manner, almost a doubling of her distress when, just after she had more or less finally convinced herself that Chloe was dead, this should happen.

'I will show her the pictures, Elaine. That's what we've got, and it would be inhuman not to share them with her. It would also be a confirmation; no one is more likely to be able to recognise the girl beyond any reasonable doubt than her mother. If there is even an iota of doubt about it, Brigitte will be able to tell us.'

'And what about tracking Chloe down, sir? How do we go about that?'

'I think I've got a good idea as to where she might have gone, but I'm not prepared to share that yet, even with you, Elaine. If she is where I think she is, I might get to talk to her on my own, but if I go there with anyone else, she may well be spooked.'

His sergeant looked a little disgruntled, but Bellamy knew there were times when that was inevitable. There were some jobs he needed to do alone.

'I'm sorry, Elaine,' he said. 'If things are as I think they are, we're looking at a difficult and possibly dangerous situation; one person is worth the risk, two is too much of a risk. But what I want you to do is at least as important as what I'm doing. I want you to take the pictures we have available and show them to Brigitte; if she confirms that the pictures are of Chloe, then we can take that as positive identification. Brigitte will not confirm them unless she is certain about it. And then I would want both you and her to wait and do nothing until you hear from me. It might be a while before you do, but nevertheless, it's vital that you stay put until I'm in touch with you. If I'm entirely wrong, I'll be in touch sooner rather than later, and if I'm right, I may need to talk to her for some time. The vital thing is that neither you nor Brigitte try and second guess me or introduce anyone else into the situation, and especially not any other members of the Manningham family, and especially, especially not Miles. I won't ask you if you're OK with that, because I can see that you're not, but that's how it needs to be.'

'Yes, sir.'

Bellamy watched her walking away, admiring her restraint and capacity to obey orders. She was a police officer to her fingertips, and if a superior officer said do it, she did it. She was probably more controlled and disciplined in that respect than he was himself, with his tendency to tell his superior officers to go to hell as long as he knew he had another decent job to go to.

He believed that Chloe was now somewhere in Aitken's Wood. If he was to go to Aitken's Wood without the express permission of the head of the Manningham household, he would technically be trespassing on Manningham property, but there were about 200 acres of Aitken's Wood, and his Scout training, long ago and far away, had been sufficient for him to ensure that no one would see him in such a space unless he wanted them to, and initially at least, he didn't want them to. The problem he had to face was that the wood was Chloe's home turf; she would know the place like the back of her hand, and if she didn't want anyone to see her in there, she was quite capable of ensuring that they didn't.

If his theorising and conjecture was anywhere near right, Chloe Manningham would also be in a highly stressed and vulnerable state of mind. He felt that she had somehow been inextricably linked to the death of her father, several weeks ago now, and the greatest weakness in his theory, the fact that she wasn't in the country, or possibly even alive, had now been disproved. She was both alive and in the country at the time of her father's death, and Bellamy felt that she was very heavily connected with it. In what capacity, he was still not sure, but he fully intended to find out.

It didn't take him long to arrive at the outskirts of the wood. It was also the edge of the Manningham estate, but the person manning the small security kiosk was young Paul Shaw. Bellamy had heard that the young man had been temporarily "demoted" by Brigitte as a warning to him to concentrate on his duties rather than spying for his father. Brigitte knew well enough that Paul tended to be more sympathetic towards the Manningham family than he was towards his father's "surveillance" ideas, and consequently she had decided it would be unfair and graceless to sack him, but he had to be made to realise where his first loyalties lay, and if a little mellow humiliation could bring that about, so much the better.

He greeted Bellamy amicably enough, which suggested that he had taken his demotion in a constructive spirit and had probably been told that it would be temporary if he behaved himself. Bellamy trusted him enough to take him a little way into his confidence, but not too far. In Bellamy's case, familiarity didn't necessarily breed contempt, but it did engender a greater professional caution.

'I don't know how long I'm going to be on the estate, Paul, and I'm afraid I'm not in a position to tell you exactly what I'm intending to do. It's enough for the moment for me to say that it is police business that I'm on, and it is also absolutely vital that I'm not interrupted for as long as I remain in the wood. I would like us to exchange our mobile numbers; if you become aware of any trespassers having gained entry to the wood, please let me know as soon as possible.'

Paul had coloured a little, and Bellamy had to tell himself to live in hope that the young man would not lose his self-control. In a few years' time, he suspected, young Paul might even make a half-decent policeman, but he had to deal with the here and now.

'What happens when you get to the end of the working day, Paul? Presumably you don't stand here all night, do you?'

'No, sir. It goes to CCTV overnight. You're not going to be in there all night, are you?'

'Not if I can help it, no. But I don't know how long this is going to take. However, don't worry, Paul. If I do have to stay in there past dark, I will phone the house and tell them what I'm doing.'

'The locals say that there is someone in there, sir.'

Bellamy took care to react nonchalantly to this, even as he emphatically noted it.

'I imagine there are always rumours that someone is in there, Paul. It's that kind of place.'

For all his police and journalistic experience of intimidating and threatening environments, Bellamy found the wood more and more menacing the further he ventured into it. Much of it was beyond pleasant, recreational forest glades; the trees, ferns and undergrowth were thick and increasingly difficult to push through, and the background miscellany of noises was not always easy to understand and interpret. Two hundred acres didn't sound particularly large as a detached, written measurement, but the reality of it was drastically different from any normal urban or suburban environment. Both the Manninghams had determined that the wood would remain, as far as was feasible, a wild environment and home to as many species of normal British wildlife creatures as possible.

Bellamy had taken the precaution of putting on wellington boots, and given the soft terrain frequently beneath his feet, it had been a sound move. He found he was gradually losing track of time as he plodded on past the various obstacles in his way. Occasional sudden scurrying noises suggested small creatures which he had only just avoided treading on, and the further he penetrated the wood, the more cacophonous and mysterious the chorus around him became, almost as if the place had a communication system of exchanged animal noises.

It registered with him that his idea of Chloe's favourite girlhood environment, which he supposed he had imagined as something equivalent to a general children's story *Swallows and Amazons* place, was actually very different, and fascinating as it must have been for her, it was also indicative of a child with more nerves and resilience than available to many of her age, girls or boys. Whoever the boys were who she condescended to allow accompany her must have been quite severely tested. Perhaps that was largely why she brought them here in the first place. Whatever they got up to and wherever that was, Chloe must have known there was absolutely no chance of anyone finding them out.

Minutes turned to hours and Bellamy's impatience with himself, never totally at rest, started increasing as he plunged awkwardly on. For all his Scout training, he knew well enough he was making enough noise to be heard from some distance away. The fact that he was younger, smaller and a lot more agile in those Scouting days he had not taken into account anything like as much as he should have done.

Passing time increased his doubts and suspicions. Chloe the girl might have been used to coming here in many different circumstances, and often when her mind was troubled and seeking escape. But, of course, the Chloe he had been told about by her relatives was mostly Chloe the girl; they had grown up with her, but whether they had had the same level of contact with her since she became an adult was more doubtful. It was not infrequently one of the disadvantages of finding out about the adult person from family whose main acquaintance with her or him had been during their childhood and adolescence. "The child is father to the man" was a misleading approach to investigations, Bellamy thought; people did change, and sometimes quite drastically. He realised he was basing his whole thinking on trying to predict Chloe's reactions to her situation as she returned home, on the picture he had built up from her relatives. Concentrating more on her friends and work colleagues might have been a better strategy.

However, stranded in Aitken's Wood and already feeling some uncertainty about whether he would be able to find his way out, there seemed little other alternative but to give his thinking a full and proper chance to be right.

And then, after a period of time which he could not possibly have quantified with any degree of accuracy, he found a small clearing in the thick woodland and for just five seconds at most, he heard a noise which he felt sure was breathing, and human breathing at that. Scouting had also taught him to distinguish between animal noise and human noise, and that swift, passing sequence of quick breaths, as muted as the owner of them could manage, signalled to him that someone was actually following him.

He sat as comfortably as he could on a fallen tree trunk and tried to stay as still as possible. The noise was not repeated, but after a period seemingly only of a few minutes, there was a crack of broken wood, no more than ten or twelve yards away on his right.

The idea that an animal might be tracking him he dismissed as highly unlikely. Whatever else might find its way into Aitken's Wood, large predatory animals would not be among them, and smaller animals would regard him very much as a creature to be avoided, even the ones of a more curious disposition.

He remained where he was for a further ten minutes, but no clear and identifiable noises were repeated. If someone was tracking him, they clearly had had some Scout training of their own. Or, he thought, trying not to dismiss the thought as wishful thinking, whoever was there knew this wood like the back of their hand.

On he plunged, now completely oblivious to where he was going. Weariness was setting in, and in time, he saw that the light was beginning to fade. He had brought a small torch with him, knowing that whatever results his expedition might achieve could take a considerable time. In his mind, the mist of doubt which he rarely allowed himself was growing by the minute, as his physical and mental discomfort made him question the whole thinking which had led him to this escapade. Chloe the girl would retreat to Aitken's Wood when her mind was troubled; Chloe the woman and sophisticated company executive would probably have found, by now, more adult and subtle refuges. He was doing that which he always most dreaded; he was making a fool of himself in front of people who trusted him, people he thought of as his clients. Chloe had returned to the country, yes; there was clear proof of that. But was there also another piece of footage, spotted by another eagle-eyed security guy, of the same woman leaving the country again, and would it take a few more weeks before that emerged, from whatever restraints the cautious senior staff were putting on it?

No, no, no. His mind rebelled against such conclusions even as it fought back against his tiredness and disillusion. The idea that Chloe, having found out about her father's death, would leave the country without making any attempt to see and console her mother, towards whom she had, he suspected, more deep-rooted affection than even her father, was just too incredible and illogical to be countenanced.

And then again that breathing noise, and this time he reacted immediately, grabbing his torch and pointing it directly at the noise. He didn't at first recognise what the light was showing him; it looked like a couple of crossed pieces of wood. He allowed the small beam to show the object from left to right, and then his heart did literally miss a beat; it was a crossbow, home-made possibly, but looking quite capable of being used as a deadly weapon. This, of course, he thought, as his immediate panic subsided, was a testament to Chloe's ingenuity; she didn't just rely on her strength of personality, or the fact that her family owned the wood, to protect her domain. She could and did arm herself.

The light beam caught a quick passing moment of part of a face, and the owner of the face clearly realised immediately that her anonymity was no more, because a voice followed within a few seconds, a voice thick with emotion and some menace.

'Who are you and what do you want?'

Bellamy held up his hands and looked round for somewhere to sit; he spotted a convenient tree trunk a few yards away.

'My name is Max Bellamy, and I'm a police inspector. I'm investigating the circumstances surrounding your father's death. Whatever happens now, Chloe, is likely to determine not just your future, but the future of your whole family, including your mother.'

'What the hell do you know about my mother?' Into the aggression and hostility of the voice had crept a note of something like appeal.

Bellamy sighed and looked at the ground around his feet. Something was scurrying away into the undergrowth.

'I know that she is almost out of her mind with grief, not only at the death of her husband, but also the as yet totally unexplained disappearance of her daughter.' He allowed a note of aggression into his own voice, calculating that this was not a woman likely to be impressed by soft soap and honeyed words.

A crossbow bolt thudded into the bark of a tree only a few feet away from him. Bellamy resolved to stay where he was, but at the same time, he was working out the distance between them and the time it would take him to cover it.

'The affairs of the Manningham family are no concern of yours, whoever you are. Get off my family's land – you're trespassing – and don't come back.'

Bellamy took his phone from his pocket.

'One of two things can happen here, Chloe,' he said. 'You can come out and talk to me, or I can call up several units of police who will have this whole wood surrounded before you have time to get out of it. If you hit me with one of those things, you will add an assault on a police officer to obstructing a police officer in the execution of his duty to your charge sheet, and rather than help your family to recover from a desperately sad, I might almost say tragic, period, you will be adding a court case to all the other family troubles.'

He heard the breathing become heavier, and he softened his tone.

'We can sort this out, Chloe. Come and talk to me. Please.'

A long, tortuous silence; Bellamy hardly dared to breathe. He heard something which sounded like a gasp or a sob. His inner radar had now pinned down exactly where she was, and he held himself ready for a final choice on a quick – a very quick – dive in her direction.

But Chloe Manningham now made herself fully visible, her eyes pausing to inspect Bellamy carefully. Something about him seemed to reassure her.

'You'll never know just how close you came,' she said, in almost a whisper.

'Can we go somewhere where we can just talk?' said Bellamy.

'So you're not summoning squads of police to carry me off?'

Bellamy grinned.

'I don't think so. Do I need to?'

'I've done nothing wrong.'

'Well, there's no reason why we can't just talk, then.'

She looked at him, and he knew this time she was looking at him in some detail. After some seconds, she turned away.

'Come with me. I have somewhere not far from here which will be much easier for talking than this place.'

She moved easily through the woodland, with Bellamy following more laboriously. After about fifteen minutes, when Bellamy was beginning to wonder whether he was heading towards some kind of trap, they came into a clearing where the undergrowth gave way to grass and a few wild flowers. At the edge of it, she had built a shelter, but it was so carefully made and disguised that Bellamy only recognised it for what it was when they were both just a few feet from the side entrance. She had supplemented the overhanging branches with wood and leaves to form a roof. Near to the shelter, but further enough away to prevent any connecting flames, she had created a firepit with the use of an empty drum from a washing machine, which told Bellamy both that some people were still illegally dumping things on the edge of the Manningham estate and that Chloe was sharp enough and organised enough to take advantage of it. A few embers were still alight in the fire, and it took Chloe only a few minutes to bring the fire up to a sufficient standard to warm the two of them as they sat on a couple of improvised wooden seats looking into the flames.

Bellamy watched her carefully as she went quietly about her business. Her easy efficiency was almost disturbing. This was a woman used to a comfortable standard of life, who had voluntarily taken to living in a wood – yes, a wood that was on her family's territory, but a wood all the same. If she had had or was having some kind of nervous breakdown, it was an extraordinarily controlled and pragmatic one. Bellamy could see enough inside the shelter to suggest that Chloe had made herself as comfortable as possible. She had been doing this in Aitken's Wood since childhood, and it seemed to come almost as second nature to her.

For the moment, she didn't seem inclined to talk. Max Bellamy was perfectly capable of recognising when things needed to be done to someone else's timescale, and for the moment at least, he held his tongue. He knew well enough that he could bring this present scene to an abrupt close whenever he decided to, but he also felt instinctively that he was now on the edge of bringing his investigation to an end, and the last thing he wanted to do was muck everything up at this late stage.

Eventually, and quite suddenly, as they were both staring hypnotically into the flames, Chloe spoke.

'So why are you here, Inspector?'

It was not an aggressive or peremptory question; it was more a registering of a gentle interest. Bellamy looked across at her, but her eyes would not meet his. Only up to a point would he allow himself to completely play someone else's game.

'I could ask you the same question. You are the chief executive of a substantial commercial corporation, and you are currently living like a Girl Guide. If anyone has questions to answer, Chloe, it's not me. You know full well why I'm here; I've already told you. I've been appointed to examine the circumstances surrounding the death of your father.'

'You must know by now, with the kind of backup you've got available, that my father died of natural causes. Why is it still any of your business?'

'It rather depends on how you define "natural causes", Chloe. Your father died from a massive heart attack, and yes, he was known to have a heart problem, but why he should have such an attack while sitting peacefully in his own study looking out at the countryside views remains an unsolved question. Police work isn't just about murders, or just about manslaughters, for that matter. Police work is about explaining unexplained happenings, particularly ones which cause suffering and distress to people, as this one has.'

To his alarm, her eyes suddenly filled with tears.

'OK, then, Inspector Nosey Parker, I'll satisfy your professional curiosity, and when I have, perhaps you can tell me, with your so logical and analytic mind, how I am supposed to live the rest of my life anywhere else but hiding in this wood trying to make sense of things.'

Bellamy had a good professional experience of knowing when to keep quiet, and he kept quiet. Chloe looked as if she was gathering her thoughts.

In a quiet and largely unemotional tone, she began her story, taking it back to the research demonstration which had resulted in such an uninhibited row with her head of research, or, as she saw it, her father's head of research. She told of her flight to France, as if a confused dream had suddenly manifested itself into real life, and her subsequent loss, right in the middle of one of the capitals of Europe, of almost all her recent memory.

'I suppose it's most like finding yourself reborn as a fully grown adult, with no proper recollection of what has happened since your birth.'

She told what she could remember of meeting Jean-Claude, and her subsequent completely mystifying trip to Jean-Claude's apartment. From then on, she said, things started to gain a momentum of their own, and she realised she had already more or less lost control of events.

As the tale continued, the hardened policeman in Bellamy was slowly giving way to the empathic investigator who needed to understand motives and means. Such a deeply alarming and devastating experience would have left many people desperate, isolated and profoundly unbalanced; this extraordinary woman had met the crisis of her life head on and actually managed to build an entirely new existence for herself.

She spoke of Jean-Claude Menteau, now fully a part of her account, with such affection and respect that the underlying truth of her experience broke right through to Bellamy. He realised that Jean-Claude was actually the only person, apart from her parents, that Chloe had ever really loved, and to find such a love, she had had to reinvent herself.

But it was as she approached the account of her return to the UK that Chloe's dispassionate account began to get markedly more heartfelt and emotional.

'I just didn't know what to do. I think I can normally see the territory around me and keep up with what's happening in it, but when I first set foot back in this country, it seemed as if I couldn't do anything else but hurt people. As soon as I got out of the airport, I thought of phoning my parents, but then the idea was suddenly terrifying; if they'd become reconciled to the idea that I wasn't coming back, that something drastic had happened to me, would they accuse me of being an impostor or something? Would they start asking me all sorts of personal questions to check on me? If I had my phone on visual, would I look as I'd always looked to them, or would they just not credit that it was really me? I thought I almost certainly must look older, after everything I've been through; my hair is different, my eyes might look different when they're peering into the phone at me. And what was I going to say? How could I begin to explain, especially over the phone, the sequence of weird events which has overtaken me since I was last in the country?

'I came to the conclusion that there really was only one way to do it. I had to go there, go and see them. Then they would be so much more likely to accept that, yes, I was their daughter Chloe, and we could take it from there. Even if my whole story sounded incredible to them, and I knew it might, they would know it was me they were talking to.

'And I decided, rightly or wrongly, that it needed to be Dad first. It was his company, in his family for generations, that I'd let down and abandoned, when in a responsible and very senior situation.

'I knew the layout of Houghton Hall, and I knew where his study was. I knew he liked to stand on the patio outside his study enjoying the country views, because those views from the hall are incredible. Even in France, such a beautiful country, I have yet to see such a view as was available from Houghton Hall. The ground from Dad's study slopes down and he can see across the country for a good three miles.'

Bellamy looked at the young woman sitting only a few feet away from him, her face now shining in the firelight, her eyes, blue as they come, glistening brightly. He thought he knew now what had happened when she had finally met her father, and he knew also that he was not too far from tears himself. Both his journalistic and his police experience had taught him that life was capable of being very cruel, but he suspected that what he was shortly about to hear would be on a level of cruelty which even he had rarely experienced before.

Chloe was looking deeply into the fire, and for a moment it seemed as if she had travelled to somewhere else and couldn't bring her mind back to the present.

When she started to speak again, her tone had softened and the anguish behind her words was so very obvious that Bellamy knew he could not even begin to doubt the truth of what she was saying.

'I thought I was being considerate. I really did. Gradually bringing myself back to him so that he would have time and leisure to get used to the idea and recover from whatever grim notions his mind had concocted of what might have happened to me.

'There's a spot on the approach road to Houghton Hall when the trees and hedges clear and you can see the whole house suddenly laid out before you. I discovered it years ago, when I was still not much more than a child. It must be about half a mile away from the hall, but you can see clearly all the way. I'd left to go to the hall very early in the morning, and everything was quiet. I pulled my car into a small lane nearby; I knew this was already on the Manningham estate, so I could just pick the car up later.

'I moved through the trees and on to the grass. I could see the window of my father's study in the distance, and the patio outside it. I started walking in the diagonal which would take me right across the field to the patio. Sometimes I stopped and waved.

'Then I saw my father emerge from his study and stand on the patio. Even at a distance, I could see that he was peering forward, as if staring into a fog, as if his eyes couldn't trust what they were showing him. I stopped and waved again.

'Suddenly, he stopped moving too, but he didn't wave back. He fell, or rather collapsed, onto the patio.'

Chloe's head sank and a long, slow wail emanated from her.

'I thought, oh God, oh God, what's happened, and I started to run. When I got to him, he was lying very still; he was deathly pale, ghastly pale. My mind was racing; I couldn't think straight; what had happened, what could I do?

'The patio door was open, and I managed to drag him back into the house; he must have been told to lose weight or something, because he just didn't seem very heavy. I succeeded in getting him back into his armchair, and I thought, well, now he's comfortable, now he's away from the cold, hard concrete of the patio, he'll wake up, he's just fainted, maybe the anxiety he's been feeling has caught up with him. He'll be alright in a minute, I thought, and we'll talk, and I'll be able to explain everything.

'But he had slumped forward onto the desk, and then something like panic set in. At the back of my mind, I knew it, I realised that he was dead, he was actually—'

Finally, a sob broke from her. For some seconds, her whole body was racked with crying. Bellamy waited; he felt as if he had suddenly been paralysed.

'Then I saw some pills on the desk. I didn't know what they were, but some idea went through my head that they might be capable of reviving him. I knew how innovative my father had always been, how receptive his mind always was to the science around him, and I had an idea that maybe these tablets were exactly what he kept here to help him when he had an attack like this. I had gloves on against the cold of the morning, but I got the little bottle open, and a few spilled out, I think; I can't remember clearly enough.

'Then I realised how stupid I was being; how could he possibly take them in the state he was in? *I've killed him, I've killed him*, it kept repeating in my mind over and over again, *I've killed my own father as a result of my stupidity and faithlessness.*

'So, I ran. It was still too early for many people to be about, and all I wanted to do was to hide myself away, not talk to anyone, not have to pretend that everything was OK, all the world was normal, when I'd just killed my own father.

'I came to Aitken's Wood, where I knew solitude would be guaranteed if I wanted it to be. Aitken's Wood was my territory, going way, way back, the place where I had discovered all kinds of things, about me, about boys, about wildlife, about nature and science. I had a crazy idea that I would just live in the wood for the rest of my life, keeping away from everyone I loved, in case my craziness caused someone else further damage.

'So, I've been here ever since. I've seen some of the comings and goings at the hall, and wondered what was going on, until it dawned on me that they would be looking for someone, and that someone would be me. I knew I couldn't even go back to Jean-Claude and our child, because the ghost of my father would be with me for ever and I would never be able to escape from what I'd done. Maybe I'm the ultimate Judas; maybe, all the way through everything, I was ultimately doomed to betray him by somehow championing the people who disagreed with him. Maybe, God help us, we are just like it, father and daughter; as he betrayed his own father, breaking the old man's heart by taking his business out of his hands, so I haven't been able to resist doing what I could to run my father's business the way I wanted it run, not the way he wanted it run. And so, I forced him to an early death, just as he did to his own father. Oh God, are we doomed to this or something? Was it always going to be like this, whatever I tried to do to escape it, even when I forgot my own life and tried to find another one?'

Chloe's eyes suddenly rested on the man sitting in front of her.

'A policeman with his eyes full of tears,' she said quietly. 'That's a new experience for me, Inspector – oh, God, what is your name? I mean, your first name?'

'Max.'

For several minutes, they sat silently together. Then Chloe spoke again, and her voice was different, as if having finally told her story, some weight had been lifted from her.

'So, what happens now, Max? Are you going to arrest me or something?'

'What for?'

'I don't know. Wasting police time. Disappearing without explanation. Faking evidence, I suppose you could say.'

Bellamy found his mouth was very dry. His words, when he found them, came out almost in a croak.

'I've listened to your story very carefully, Chloe, and I think I have as competent an understanding of the law as I need to do my job. As far as I can see, the only clear breakage of the law you have committed is entering the country under a false passport, though even then a defence lawyer could make a tenable case for saying that your married name has replaced your maiden name; I suspect not many prosecuting counsel would be all that happy to go ahead with the case. What happened with your father was, in the last analysis, an accident; your father had a weak heart to begin with, I think partly because he had left it too long to do something about, and your motives for going to him in the way you did were entirely understandable, even if they did prove to be mistaken. The important thing now is for your family to begin the process of putting your lives back together. You need to leave here now and go to Houghton Hall; I will phone ahead, if you wish, to make sure your mother has some knowledge of what has happened. She knows my voice well enough now, and if it's me, you can avoid the problems you were worried about. Your mother is, in any case, a more phlegmatic and adaptable character than your father was, if you'll forgive me saying so. I have met your father on a few occasions, and I'm not trying to denigrate him in any way; he was a remarkably gifted man. But we are all human and vulnerable, and he had been in a pressurised occupation for a long time.'

Bellamy made himself stop. Cleaning up processes tended to make him impatient, since they usually tended to make all the clearer the mess which events and people had combined to bring about. Chloe had been staring at him all the time he was speaking, and for a moment, he expected some flat refusal, or some long-winded rebuttal of what he saw as needing to happen. But it seemed as though she had just been assimilating his words.

'Mr Put-It-Right. Yes, I suppose all that can be done now. And I must, of course, get in touch with Jean-Claude. I deliberately didn't give him any contact numbers because, when all's said and done, what could they have been? If he'd contacted Houghton Hall before they knew where I was, the whole thing could have blown up in my face. The poor man must be going out of his mind by now. Oh, Max, I've been living in some sort of a bad dream, haven't I? Except the worst bits were actually real.'

Bellamy took his phone from his pocket.

'Shall I? I'm not going to contact the hall until you agree that I can, Chloe.'

She glanced down into the fire for several seconds. Then she looked back at him and nodded.

'Yes, it's time this all came to an end.'

Sometimes, Bellamy thought, *there's no alternative but to push your luck.*

'Brigitte may want to talk to you on the phone, Chloe. Are you up for that?'

For a moment, something like panic crossed Chloe's face. Then she looked into the fire again, which seemed to be providing her with some kind of inspiration.

'Yes, OK, Max, let's do it. Mum first, but then it has to be Jean-Claude.'

Bellamy knew the number off by heart by now. The familiar voice had the tone it usually had these days; quizzical, slightly bored, verging on irritation.

'Brigitte, you would do well to sit down, I think.'

'Why? What? Don't pay bloody games with me, Max. I don't play these days—'

'I have someone here who would like to speak to you, and it's someone you perhaps didn't expect to speak to again. Now please, Brigitte, sit down and take a few deep breaths; there's been enough trouble, and we don't want any more.

'You mean…'

Bellamy carried the phone to Chloe and handed it over. He moved himself to a discreet distance, but he could still hear the shriek Brigitte made when she heard who she was talking to.

These moments, Bellamy thought, *these moments are what this job is all about. Yes, there's all the stuff about solving puzzles, understanding people, interpreting motives, but outcomes like this are not just the icing on the cake, they are the cake.*

Now it was a question of doing all the right things in the right order. After Chloe had been made to promise faithfully that she would leave Aitken's Wood and make her way to the hall as soon as she had talked to her husband, and the husband bit took nearly fifteen minutes all on its own, a second phone call followed the first, and the shriek made by Jean-Claude, male as it was, could match the earlier shriek for volume and passion.

Bellamy was registering a few relevant points, even as he

waited for Chloe to finish talking to whoever she wanted to talk to. Firstly, Elaine had already been in touch with the hall, giving them very guarded updates on what had been happening, and it sounded as if Elaine was actually at the hall now.

Which Bellamy saw as good news, even if Elaine could be said to have technically exceeded her brief. Bellamy, however, was grateful to her once more for acting on her own initiative. As usual at the end of a case, he was weary and in need of his own company, and Elaine was probably better qualified than he was to see the mother and daughter reconciliation through to the new beginning it needed to make.

Left to himself, Bellamy might have spent hours, if not days, finding his way out of Aitken's Wood, but Chloe, of course, knew exactly where she was, and she had no need to return to the security gate and Paul Shaw. Bellamy was quite pleased with the young man for a change; he had done what he'd been told to do, but there would be time to deal with all that later. Chloe's exit from the wood was only a few hundred yards away from the back entrance to Houghton Hall, and there was Brigitte, alongside Elaine, looking out from exactly the right window and waving frantically.

Bellamy could claim long experience of knowing the appropriate moments to make himself scarce, but he was not prepared to spare himself the satisfaction of seeing mother and daughter reunited. To watch Brigitte's legendary composure and control break down so thoroughly only emphasised how iron her will was to begin with. Having lost her husband, one of the two most precious people in her life, to come to a realisation that she was not now going to lose the other one was enough to sweep away her carefully nurtured cosmopolitan sophistication altogether. Bellamy was watching two women renewing a precious relationship that both had feared lost for ever, and while he could not help experiencing faint sensations of voyeurism, he also felt a decided glow of triumph that he had been instrumental in bringing it about.

After five minutes of reunion, both women realised that Bellamy was still there, standing discreetly outside the entrance to the house. They released each other, and both sets of eyes turned in Bellamy's direction, with a third pair belonging to Elaine joining them a few seconds later.

Their looks spoke of something very intense and very heartfelt. Bellamy felt as if he was somehow naked before them and they were inspecting his entire being, both physical and mental. His own sangfroid was momentarily and highly unusually shaken.

'Perhaps it's time we pushed off and left these good ladies in peace, Elaine,' he said, almost hesitantly.

Inevitably, it was Brigitte who broke the spell. She walked up to him and kissed him lightly on both cheeks.

'I can work most men out, but I'm still thinking about you. Whatever it is that makes you tick, Max, whatever mysterious spirit informs your ability to act on your hunches and spread peace and light around you, please understand that for ever afterwards you will always be welcome in this house, day or night, summer or winter. And if that idiot Gregson has anything further to say, please refer him to me personally and I will take a vicarious delight in flattening him and dancing on his bones.'

Somehow, Elaine had positioned herself next to him. Not unusually for him in moments of high emotion, he all but dried up. But enough words emerged, albeit tentatively.

'It was my pleasure, Brigitte. And when you and Chloe have picked the pieces up and put everything back together, I would love to come back and see you again.'

'That's a definite, Max. I imagine you've already heard the full story – well, you must have done, having spent so much time with Chloe. I'm looking forward to hearing it, and then we'll be looking to make contact with whoever is on Chloe's list for contact. Soon, we'll have the whole family as it is now back together, and wherever Ralph is now, I'm sure that will afford him the peace he deserves.'

As their car made its way out of Houghton Hall's grounds, a phone sounded. Elaine answered it.

'Yes, sir. He's next to me. He's driving at the moment, sir. Yes, I'll ask him.'

'It's DCS Gregson, sir. He wants to talk to you. Shall I arrange it for later?'

Bellamy smiled.

'No, Elaine. Put me on hands free. I'll talk to DCS Gregson.'

PART FIVE

AFTERMATH

This time, DCS Gregson detected the political ring, but realised that, for once, it didn't unduly disturb his peace of mind. Retirement was only just round the corner now, and short of some sudden and unforeseen cataclysm, he would soon be enjoying relaxed beaches and leisurely countryside outings, and people like Mr. Coulson would just be big, bad bogies of the past. He might even, he thought, put a Coulson face on the inside door of his shed and practise his darts on it.

'Well, Detective Chief Superintendent Gregson, how are you this splendid morning? Splendid, I hasten to add, not in the meteorological sense – when is it in this country? – but one of those rare occasions when we can look at a largely untroubled horizon.'

'I'm well, thank you, Mr. Coulson, as you appear to be.'

'Yes, indeed. The Elevated Ones, those whose names we can only speak with awe, are happily reconciled to recent events. Your man – Bellamy, isn't it – has finally delivered the goods, and the Elevated have heard and are at peace. We are now out of the territory of one of our prominent donors having topped himself because he had been doing drugs, or cavorted with ladies of the night, or buggered local choirboys; he was simply a decent guy whose dodgy ticker couldn't cope with his long-lost daughter, who he believed to be dead, suddenly strolling towards him through the morning mist. Your man took rather longer than the Elevated, in their omnipotent wisdom, would prefer, but he stuck commendably to his guns and all is well. We must take steps. What is Bellamy at the moment?'

'What is he? A policeman and ex-journalist – I'm not sure what you mean.'

'I mean what rank is he, Gregson? Do try to keep up. You're not drawing the pension cheques quite yet.'

'Oh. He's an inspector.'

'Well, before you swan off to Benidorm or wherever else suits your leisure habits, make him a chief inspector. You can assume you're a Royal or something, or even the PM, giving people gongs when your own day is done. We can probably give that sergeant of Bellamy's a leg up too – the one who's in all the press pictures, looking fiercely maternal.'

'Thank you, sir. I'm sure that will be most appreciated.'

'So it should be, Gregson. It's not often that we sanction a double bunk up the greasy pole. Let's hope the now Chief Inspector Bellamy will have tact enough to follow up his Manningham triumph with others of an equal ilk.'

Gregson secretly hoped likewise, but unlike his political master, he had actually met and crossed swords with the inspector already, and he wasn't so sure that Bellamy would be any more conveniently obedient in the future than he had been in the past. Bellamy was one of the individuals capable of troubling him, and he had determined that, as far as possible, his remaining working days would be as harmonious and unclouded as possible. He intended to avail himself of one of the advantages of rank and give the job of telling Bellamy the news to Tom Hollins, who appeared to be on the Bellamy wavelength. Perhaps some time in the future, he thought, Bellamy the independent thinker, the man who did it his way regardless of what others, including his superiors, thought about it, might be sitting in the very chair Gregson was occupying now, with results which could prove to be very interesting. How, he wondered, would Bellamy cope with the odious Coulson? How would Bellamy tell his subordinates to do what he wanted them to do, regardless of what they themselves wanted to do? Every maverick has to face the system eventually; every loose cannon sooner or later has to have his gun spiked. Collins could do the job of telling the now undoubtedly insufferably smug Bellamy about his promotion, and while he was on the subject, Gregson thought, there might just be a fair few other troublesome tasks which he could unload on to various underlings to smooth his way to the great day.

Some irritating little demon inside him was whispering that unloading troublesome tasks on to subordinates was more or less what he'd been doing ever since he came into his present high and mighty status, but Gregson rapidly repressed the thought, with a creepy suspicion that perhaps the omni-talented Bellamy even had telepathic powers. He pulled himself together and told another subordinate to get Detective Superintendent Hollins on the phone.

Max Bellamy was in his study several hours later, thoughtfully inspecting the current plans for the next county-lines drugs seizure. He thought the general strategy of the raid was sound enough, but it seemed to him that too much attention had been concentrated on preparing the operation and not enough had been given to ensuring that the raid was on the right place. Nothing would make the force look sillier that to mount an extravagant raiding party on the wrong house.

Undercover officers were generally to be avoided, in Bellamy's opinion, because the use of them could very easily go badly wrong, but sometimes the range of choices was narrow. He sat in his armchair with a pencil hovering about his lips and tried once again to stop the Manninghams breaking in on his contemplations.

And, at that precise moment, the phone rang. Bellamy thought it must inevitably be one of the Manninghams, given his train of thought, but it turned out to be Tom Hollins.

'Detective Superintendent Hollins, good to hear from you, sir. What particular pile of excrement is now about to fall on my head?'

'You're a born pessimist, aren't you, Max? It's actually good news I have for you.'

'Now I really am terrified.'

'You will, very shortly, become Detective Chief Inspector Bellamy. Gregson has had a call from Olympia, or more specifically, the politico Coulson, and the Immortals have decreed that you should go up a notch, being as they're so generally chuffed that you've settled the Manningham case without landing them all in the clarts.'

'Bloody hell.'

'I take it that is an expression of pleasure, Chief Inspector?'

'I suppose so. It's just that I've always been a bit wary of how far up the greasy pole it's advisable to go. I don't much want to finish up where Gregson is, sitting in a big office with his thumb up his bum while everyone else runs around doing the work.'

'A graphic image of our Big Chief Gregson, young man. Dammit, Max, you're a weird bastard at times. Can't you be happy that you're managing to fool most of the people most of the time?'

'If you say so. I just remember the editors I've worked with; journalism and the police are not so wildly different as you might think. I've known some real greats, but their jobs were about sitting around in offices telling other people what to do, which other people didn't always do. I like to be out there, moving about in the real world. And it's all a bit fickle, isn't it, Tom? A few weeks back, I wasn't far away from being out on my arse.'

Bellamy could only hear a long sigh at the other end of the line.

'Listen to me, Maximilian Bellamy, you contrary bugger. You were a good journalist, and now you're a good policeman. And there's no great mystery to it, when push comes to shove. You do the job, you follow up the leads, you check all the exits, you take your hunches out and inspect them up and down before acting on the one which makes most sense. But there's still that nagging doubt in there, isn't there, Max? I don't know where it's from, maybe one of your parents, maybe a few disasters when you were still sorting yourself out, maybe you're just not given to patting yourself on the back. Yes, sure, you're not the kind of guy who would have made it through the ranks once upon a time, when it's all kiss-sir's-arse, spit and polish, Freemason handshakes or whatever the hell they shake. But the fact that a one-off like you can make his way shows how policing is changing; not all of it is for the better, you know that as well as I do, but some of it is. Hang in there, DCI Bellamy, for all our sakes, including yours, even if you don't always think so.'

Bellamy was chastened and heartened at the same time. He realised he was smiling into the phone.

'Thanks, Tom. I appreciate it. But what about Elaine?'

'Elaine goes up a step too. You're going to be a power couple; all the bad guys will be dust beneath your chariot wheels. Now go do whatever you do to celebrate, and no, don't tell me what it is, because I probably wouldn't believe you.'

'I'll tell Louise. Nurse's uniform and enema kit on hold.'

When the call finished, Bellamy sat very still for a few minutes. He could hear Louise moving about downstairs. He grinned to himself and went down to tell her the news.

Three weeks and two days after Max Bellamy and Chloe Manningham walked out of Aitken's Wood, the board of the Manningham Corporation met for the first time since Ralph Manningham's death. The grand boardroom, all dark wood and big windows, was hushed as if many of the thirty-three people assembled around the central table still couldn't fully believe recent events.

The high-backed chairman's chair was occupied by Brigitte Manningham (née Lacoste), and her assumption of the chair didn't seem to strike anyone as at all out of place. If she was nervous, she wasn't showing it; her intelligent, rather quizzical eyes were concentrated at first on the document in front of her. When she spoke, it was with an easy, relaxed tone, loud enough to reach everyone around the table but not loud enough to sound like the teacher in front of the class.

'Ladies and Gentlemen,' she said. 'It is exactly ten-thirty, and we will start as we mean to go on in terms of observing the punctuality of meetings.'

A few furtive whisperings immediately ceased.

'This is the first time the board has met since the untimely death of my dear husband, Ralph, the last chairman of the Manningham Corporation. I want to express my personal gratitude and that of the Manningham family for the commiserations and good wishes we have been receiving, many of them I know emanating from people round this table.'

The only other members of the Manningham family present, Brigitte's stepson, Miles, and her brother-in-law, Philip, had positioned themselves halfway down the table on either side of Brigitte, the family having made a conscious decision not to all sit themselves at the front like some controlling dynasty, even if that's exactly what they were.

'At my husband's funeral, we heard many very moving and eloquent tributes to him and it's not my intention to continue in that vein now; we have a good deal of business to attend to after our recent circumstances have made it impossible for us to have a board meeting for over three months.

'I'm going to take the minutes of our last meeting as read; they did go out some days ago, along with a particular request that any matters arising should be notified to me in advance of this meeting, and none have.

'As you probably already know from our friends in the media, I am Ralph's sole heir and his will also expressed his wish that I should take over as chairman of the board, at least for the time being. As the Manningham family retain the majority shareholding in the company, I am therefore assuming the responsibility of being chairperson of the board for the time being.

'You will be aware that one crucial member of the family is not with us today. My daughter, Chloe, has had a traumatic time of it, both on the occasion of her father's death and subsequently. She has a husband and a young son in France, and it has been decided, in accordance with her own wishes, that she returns to her family for the time being so that she can have a settled and unpressurised time to reflect and determine where and how she wants to continue her life in the future.'

Brigitte sighed, and her tone slowed.

'There is no point in denying that Chloe and her father had fundamental differences concerning the present and future of this organisation, and where it should most urgently concentrate its efforts. You are all well enough aware of the issues as they have been raised. Chloe is anxious that she doesn't win the argument simply by default, and she fears that the sympathy factor might cause the board to come down on her side and agree to her proposals for fear of causing further upset and conflict. She thinks, and I agree with her, that we are in need of a "cooling down" period, to assimilate the loss of Ralph and try to arrive at objective understandings of what we believe to be best for the corporation. We all know well enough the differences in approach and emphasis which can arise between generations, and while Chloe is still working through the guilt she feels about her differences of opinion with her father, she cannot bring herself to simply abandon her ideas about the most vital priorities simply because her father can no longer argue with her.

'That is as much as I feel it appropriate to say about the present situation of the Manningham family. We have been through a lot in the last year, in particular the last six months, but this company isn't just about the Manningham family, and I know we have a number of matters, both administrative and financial, that need our attention quite urgently now. But first, I would ask you to confirm me in the position of chairperson, for the time being at least. I am proposed by Miles Manningham and seconded by Philip Manningham. I did ask you in writing when the agenda was distributed to notify me of any other candidates who would wish to stand; we remain committed to keeping this organisation as democratic as it can be given that it is and always has been a family business. I haven't been notified of any other candidates, so I would ask you now to indicate your consent for me to temporarily take the chairmanship of this company.'

A loud series of "ayes" and "yeses" from the board members both heartened and encouraged Brigitte. She knew that what she had just done had some of the characteristics of a *coup d'*état, but she had taken pains, in the letter sent out accompanying the agenda, to emphasise that an election would be called if anyone cared to propose and second an alternative candidate, and no one's name had been put forward. She suspected that, should her chairmanship not go as smoothly as she would like it to, someone in due course would undoubtedly point out that she was elected without opposition or a proper election, but she had determined to cross that bridge when she came to it.

The meeting passed on smoothly enough to the nitty and gritty of running the company, and it became obvious, not only to Brigitte but to everyone else around the table, that her political experience had been adequate enough preparation for her current role. She knew how to keep the meeting constructive and avoid the windbags and swollen egos taking the business over, and as the board members realised her competence and, when it had to be, her toughness, an increasingly businesslike atmosphere took over in the room.

It took nearly five hours altogether, with a one-hour adjournment for lunch, to cover the outstanding matters, but Brigitte was able to heave a long sigh of relief as the meeting eventually wound up. She turned to her phone and texted a succinct message to Chloe in France: *Keeping the chair nice and warm for you, darling. All quite fun really.*

Chloe, sitting in the sunshine of her garden in Marseilles, smiled. Already, her mind seemed to be clearing from the perpetual fog of confusion and self-doubt which had been dominating it for longer than she cared to remember.

It was a beautiful day, and her south-facing garden was luxuriously bathed in sunshine. In his well-appointed pram, her son clearly enjoyed the light and colours all around him. Gurgling away happily, he occasionally broke off to look at his mother, and one of these looks, which seemed to linger for a while, suddenly reminded Chloe forcefully of the person she had lost. None of her French friends had ever met Ralph Manningham, so any resemblance the baby might bear to him would not be something they would notice, but Chloe had already noticed, and there was nothing fanciful in what she saw. The child had observable physical traces of both his parents, but those piercing blue-green eyes and the long Roman nose were absolutely pure Ralph Manningham.

The boy's eyes seemed to be examining her intently, and then, quite suddenly, a broad smile broke over his face, and the resemblance to his grandfather seemed momentarily more precise than ever.

Maybe it was her imagination. Maybe whatever she wanted to see she made herself see, but the look and the smile had such a hint of forgiveness and such an emphasis on pure love that she had to turn away in case her son saw his mother's tears.

Four weeks later, Max Bellamy found himself standing in a draughty hall in a Midlands town which was near to Louise's birthplace, if completely new to him. The election candidates were lining up on the platform, and a man much less astute than Bellamy would have worked out some three hours ago who had won. The by-election had come as something of a surprise, as the sitting MP, not of Louise's party, had finally succumbed to the bad health which had been plaguing him for some time and decided to retire, much to the irritation of his party whips, but he himself was too ill to care about them any longer.

The fact that Louise's chance had come sooner rather than later was another tremor in the foundations of Bellamy's private life, but, as usual, he had coped with it. Somewhat to his surprise, it became clear that Louise now regarded him as an electoral asset, and he had dutifully grinned and chatted to order on several public occasions as Louise wooed her prospective constituents.

It was now nearly three o'clock in the morning. Louise had gone through doubt, anxiety, an attack of indignation when a number of ballot boxes took longer than expected to appear, gradual relaxation, and eventually triumph, as it became clear that she had not only turned over her predecessor's 14,000-odd majority but had done it by a majority of her own now running on to nearly 7,000.

As the candidates stood waiting for the returning officer, a man whose generous girth did not seem to indicate the jolliness often associated with fat men, Louise's beaming smile made it all too abundantly obvious who had won. Max had been through the whole gamut of his wife's emotions throughout her campaign, including her fury at some negative coverage – "bloody fascist agitators – no wonder you got out of journalism, Max" – her pleasure at any embarrassment of her opponents – "I bet she wished now she hadn't said that, the silly woman" – and her occasional deep frustration at the reactions of voters she met on the campaign trail – "they're so vacuous I swear they haven't watched a proper news bulletin in years". As the campaign was nearing its end, she'd remarked to her husband that "now you know what it's like living with you on a complicated case", and he had noted and assimilated the remark, even if he had his doubts about being able to improve himself.

He noted, irrelevantly, that the big red rosette his wife was wearing really didn't suit her, and at last the returning officer had waddled his way to the microphone to confirm what everyone in the hall already knew, that Louise Bellamy was now this constituency's new Member of Parliament. Previous knowledge didn't stop a huge howl of delight emerging from the red ranks standing only yards from the platform.

As he watched his wife's moment of triumph, a great wave of love and pleasure swept down from Bellamy's head to the toes of his feet, and on its way past his crotch, it reminded him of one form of celebration which wouldn't be too long in arriving, because he knew Louise very well, and the glint in her eye was already very obviously there.

On the first day off suitable for the purpose, Max Bellamy made the journey that he'd promised himself ever since the conclusion of the Manningham case. Ed Mowbray and his "Judas gene" theory had returned to him again, and it became suddenly necessary, for no reason that he could define precisely, to go to the place with the last physical evidence of the life of his own father, Richard.

The care home where Richard Bellamy breathed his last was still there, though Bellamy noticed immediately a handsome new extension and even more carefully tended grounds. Bearing in mind the kind of money it cost for people to come here, luxurious grounds were probably the least that their families could expect.

Bellamy remembered the heavy ache on his heart as he parked his car. This, he thought, would be difficult; this was something he didn't want to do but had to do, a situation he was more used to in his professional life than his personal.

Richard Bellamy was of the hippie generation, and the 1967 summer of love had been perhaps the apex of his younger life. In those days, he became and remained a member of CND. Throughout the miners' strikes of the seventies and eighties, he carried banners and organised petitions. In the university where he eventually worked, he was in trouble on more than one occasion for his overt sympathies with student protests, something university lecturers were constantly "advised", as in "told", to keep clear of.

His son's entry into journalism, rather than the teaching which he probably would have preferred, he had eventually accepted but not without a series of caustic remarks about "tabloidism", "the Murdoch shilling", "sensationalist claptrap, etc.". But when Max's name started appearing on local leading articles, a kind of grudging pride set in.

Now Max was coming to tell him that he had decided to join the police force, the very mob who had carried Richard bodily away from some of his protests, the very crew he had railed against and condemned in perpetuity for their conduct against the miners. It would be like telling George Orwell, one of his father's idols and icons, that his son had just been elected to be the member for a particularly safe Home Counties Tory constituency.

Richard was sitting in his favourite armchair, looking out over the Somerset countryside. Every visit now, Max thought, the old man looked thinner, his long, exhausted features taking on ever more precisely the paleness and immobility of a death mask.

Max played for time and had almost convinced himself that he didn't really need to tell the old man yet, but then he remembered again what he termed "the blabbermouth tendency" in the Bellamy family and their associates. He could not bear to back away from it, only to find that someone else had told Richard themselves.

'Change of career, Dad, as of, what is it, two months now? Direct entry to the CID. Now when I track them down, I might just be able to put them away as well. Doing my bit to keep Joe Public safe and sound in his own sweet home.'

It was the kind of loaded silence which had once characterised a meeting when his father had discovered that Max had lied to him; Max had been about twelve at the time. Corporal punishment, even in its mildest manifestations, was anathema to Richard Bellamy, but the set of his face and the grating of his voice made more overt punishment necessary.

'You must do what you think necessary, Max,' the thin voice eventually announced. 'It is not my way, never was and never will be, certainly not now, but I've made my choices; yours are still to be made. I only hope it turns out to be the right one.'

This speech, remarkably long for his father at the time, was followed shortly afterwards by a protracted burst of coughing which eventually needed a nurse to be summoned.

In his mirror, Bellamy had seen the tears in his eyes as he started up his car. *Mowbray's Judas gene right enough, I suppose*, he thought. 'But maybe, just maybe, he's wrong and I'm right. For me, anyway,' he said aloud.

As he drove away, he was already beginning to question why he and Louise had remained childless, even though he knew it was mostly because of Louise's problems in that department. He'd always suspected that those problems could be solved with sufficient determination and expense, and maybe he and Louise were just too busy and involved to take on the time and effort of children.

Or maybe he was afraid of himself being on the end of the Judas gene. Maybe he could only too easily visualise the day when his son or daughter came to wherever he was scheduled to be in his declining years and told him their intention of doing something, personally or professionally, which would go against everything he had ever practised or believed.

But then again, he thought, perhaps it is the natural order of things. If each generation replicated the previous one, if each succeeding offspring determined to work in the same occupation, doing the same things in the same way with the same assumptions informing them, how was the world ever to move forward? And if Armageddon really was only just around the corner, new thinking and new answers would be more necessary than they had ever been.

And perhaps it was a mercy and a release that he personally would never really know.